She felt warmth spreading through her body. . . .

He stood watching her, not coming closer, as if he were afraid she would run away from him if he startled her. Her heart that she had hardened against him fluttered and started beating wildly. Still afraid of the hurt he could inflict on her if she let him know how vulnerable she was, she looked down, the curtain of her hair descending to shield her face. Then he was beside her. She was enfolded in his strong arms in the throbbing night and she had lost all awareness of the passing time. . . .

Bantam Circle of Love Romances
Ask your bookseller for the books you have missed

Dear Friend,

Enter the Circle of Love—and travel to faraway places with romantic heroes . . .

We read hundreds of novels and, each month, select the very best—from the finest writers around the world—to bring you these wonderful love stories . . . stories that let *you* share in a variety of beautiful romantic experiences.

With Circle of Love Romances, you treat yourself to a romantic holiday—anytime, anywhere. And because we want to please you, won't you write and let us know your comments and suggestions?

Meanwhile, welcome to the Circle of Love—we don't think you'll ever want to leave!

Best,
CATHY CAMHY
Editor

CIRCLE OF LOVE ™

Aloha, My Love

Lucinda Day

BANTAM BOOKS
TORONTO · NEW YORK · LONDON · SYDNEY

ALOHA, MY LOVE
A Bantam Book/July 1982

ISBN 0-553-21517-5

Published simultaneously in the United States and Canada

*Bantam Books are published by Bantam Books, Inc. Its
trademark, consisting of the words "Bantam Books" and the
portrayal of a rooster, is Registered in U.S. Patent and
Trademark Office and in other countries. Marca Registrada.
Bantam Books, Inc., 666 Fifth Avenue, New York, New York
10103.*

PRINTED IN THE UNITED STATES OF AMERICA

0 9 8 7 6 5 4 3 2 1

One

"Aloha . . . and have a nice day."

"Thank you," said Sylvie Brooke, rushing out of the employment agency and closing the door behind her.

The irony of the receptionist's lilting farewell was too much, and Sylvie yielded to the discouragement she had restrained through all the fruitless job interviews. How could she have a nice day when no one had offered the kind of job she'd spent the past four years preparing for?

Oh, this last employment counseler, Mrs. Dutton, had talked an encouraging game. That was her business. But apparently Honolulu held no need for inexperienced medical technologists like Sylvie, who had come straight from the University of Oklahoma, degree and registry in hand, thinking she would find her dream career in Hawaii. With loans to repay for her training, she couldn't afford to get trapped in some temporary, routine position. She shouldn't have believed the promises in Debbie Leighter's letters.

Her best friend, a year older, had been the lucky one—she had come last summer and gotten established.

With a soft Hawaiian breeze tossing her long, silky blond hair, Sylvie hurried along the second-floor gallery. Then, blindly turning a corner to descend the stairs, she gasped. Her face jarred into a man's chest and she dropped her clutch purse, the contents of which spilled everywhere. In numbed fascination, she watched her billfold fly out through the wrought-iron railing and drop down onto the bed of a pickup truck that was inching forward in the late-afternoon traffic.

The tall, suntanned man she had collided with bolted down the steps, shouting over his shoulder, "Why don't you use those big brown eyes to look where you're going?" before disappearing below.

Sylvie leaned over the railing and caught sight of him. His casually styled black hair looked iridescent in the afternoon sun, and he towered above the brightly dressed office workers leaving their buildings. Then he reached over the bed of the pickup, which had stopped at a traffic signal, and retrieved her billfold.

As Sylvie began to collect the scattered contents of her purse, Mrs. Dutton and the receptionist hurried along the gallery toward her, on their way home. The receptionist stopped and offered to help, but Sylvie had almost finished gathering her keys, compact, and comb, and was moving back toward the closed employment agency after a lipstick that had rolled farther.

From where she knelt on the tiled floor of the gallery, Sylvie suddenly became aware of beige slacks planted beside her, unmoving. Her gaze continued up beyond a pastel-striped shirt, open at the neck, a firm jaw, and an unsmiling mouth. With a jolt, she met the most startling eyes she had encountered in her twenty-two years. Those eyes, blue-green as the waves pounding the beaches of Oahu, pounded their displeasure into her consciousness.

Sylvie rose slowly and tilted her head to look up into the stranger's frowning face. He held out her brown leather billfold with the tooled S that Fred Barton had brought her from Mexico. "Here," he said brusquely. "I assume the S stands for *Scatterbrained*?" He turned and tried the locked door of the employment agency.

"No, it stands for *Sorry*," Sylvie murmured to his back. "Thank you for getting this back for me."

He scowled. "I had to see Mrs. Dutton and now it's too late." Without another word, he strode away.

Standing where he had left her, Sylvie absently traced the S on her billfold with her thumb. It wasn't fair for any man to be so handsome. But, as Grandma Brooke used to say, pretty is as pretty does. This man was rude and had shouted at her. *Well,* she thought, *he did get my billfold back for me, but he didn't have to act as if I made him miss Mrs. Dutton on purpose. It wasn't my fault any more than his.*

Resting her elbows on the railing and looking down the palm-lined avenue, Sylvie wondered why that stranger, so helpful but so abrupt, had been in such a hurry. He might need a job as much as she did, although he was well dressed and appeared to be in his early thirties—old enough to have established a career. Sylvie watched him stride through the crowd below, enter a parking lot, and climb into a white Jaguar.

Anyone who owned a Jaguar needed no sympathy, Sylvie thought, smoothing the skirt of her coral dress. So much for that incident, and for her second day of job hunting. She ran down the stairway and joined the crowd at the bus stop.

The incongruity of the old New England–style house surrounded by palm trees and bright tropical flowers struck Sylvie each time she crossed the broad lawn and followed the path back to the carriage house that her friend had rented. Debbie, whose father was a career Air Force officer, had lived in Hawaii as a child. She loved the islands, and after graduation a year ago, she had headed for Honolulu like a homing pigeon and found a job as a medical technologist in a hospital.

Her letters had offered a siren song of tropical glamour, glistening beaches, and exciting opportunities. "You'll love the carriage house I've found," she'd written early in the spring. "It has a lot more charm than the condominiums bordering my backyard—not that we could afford one of them! I'm afraid the developers will tear down this old place someday, but in the meantime we can pretend we have our own estate." The ground floor was a catch-all for old lawn mowers, tricycles, rusted bed springs, and a jumble of odds and ends, visible through windows that looked as if they hadn't been washed since the days of the missionaries. Debbie, with her usual flair, had made the upstairs apartment livable and attractive.

As always when Sylvie returned to these shaded grounds from job hunting, her weariness slipped away and she imagined she had stepped into a fairy tale. The soft July air was fragrant, and an exotic tropical bird trilled its song among the crimson clusters of the shower tree by the stairs leading up to the apartment. Debbie's blue Monza, parked in the shade, would carry them off to romantic adventures here in these enchanted islands.

Oklahoma was never like this! Sylvie thought. Neither was Fred. Sweet, earnest Fred Barton, who was waiting back home for her to get "this foolishness" out of her system while he clerked in a prestigious law firm and studied for the bar exam. Despite her mother's reminders that a promising young lawyer was a fine catch for any girl and shouldn't be kept dangling, Sylvie couldn't help wondering whether she was ready to marry him and settle into a life as flat as an Oklahoma wheat field. If only he would do something dashing, like sweeping her into his arms and giving her a masterful ultimatum, or . . . rushing to rescue her billfold from the back of a truck! But the blue-green eyes of her dream prince would not be contemptuous like those of the rude stranger she had just encountered.

Slowly climbing the stairs, Sylvie stopped and idly touched a delicate flower of the jade vine whose leaves covered the railing, disguising the fact that the white paint was peeling.

"Come on in, Syl! Are you going to stand out there all night?" Debbie called.

When Sylvie sauntered inside, Debbie's pixie face looked puzzled. "Are you all right? Any luck today?"

"Afraid not." Sylvie sighed. "It's the same old story—'try us again later.' What happens now? I can't sponge off you forever." She dropped into the bentwood rocker in the small living room, kicked off her dress pumps, and began rocking mechanically.

"I'm not worried." Debbie grinned. "Just relax and have some iced tea. I fixed a big pitcher, and I got some fortune cookies on the way home.''

Sylvie smiled in spite of herself. ''Fun,'' she said, reaching for the basket Debbie had set on the glass-topped coffee table.

''No you don't,'' Debbie protested, handing her a frosty glass. ''Tea first—I put mint in it like your mom used to back home. And you have to tell me all about your day. Then we'll read our fortunes and pretend they really mean something.'' Debbie arranged herself cross-legged on the bright Hawaiian-print floor cushion and looked up at her friend expectantly.

A trade wind, sweet with the fragrance of flowers, stirred the sheer café curtains at the double windows. Sylvie sighed again. ''I've been all over,'' she said. ''I went to two hospitals, filled out all the applications, and was practically told not to call them, they'd call me. Then I went to three employment agencies. All they had were clerical jobs.''

''You don't want something like that.''

''No. I didn't spend four years studying for a dead-end job. Mom would be so disappointed. You know how hard she worked after Dad died. She was determined I'd get through school and have an easier life than she's had.''

''I really admire your mother,'' Debbie said. ''It's great to know she's happy now, finally married again and with you off her hands.'' When Sylvie made a face at her, she added, ''You know I didn't mean that! But what about the med-tech job you saw in Sunday's want-ads?''

Sylvie swirled the ice in her glass, then suddenly exploded, ''I can't believe I was so dumb! They hired someone Monday morning. I should've interviewed for that one right away instead of going sightseeing and taking surfing lessons. But it seemed so good to unwind after studying for the registry exam.'' Sylvie looked at her friend in despair. ''What am I going to do now?''

''Don't panic, Syl. I thought your game plan was to relax for a few days, then look for a job— and that's exactly what you've been doing.''

Sylvie nodded, savoring the cool, minty tea. ''I wish the job at your hospital had come up, the way we counted on.''

''That Mary Ruth!'' Debbie exclaimed. ''When I called you and said to come to Hawaii right away, she'd told me she was giving her notice this week. Something about her family needing her back on the mainland.''

''It's okay, Deb, you couldn't help it.''

''She seemed so serious, and her job would've been perfect for you. How was I to know she'd fall madly in love last weekend and decide to stay awhile longer. And after I dragged you all the way here!''

''I didn't *have* to come.'' Sylvie should have known better than to count on Debbie to find her a job. Debbie's greatest charm was her irrepressible enthusiasm, but sometimes that very enthusiasm made her unreliable. Still, if Sylvie could hang on a little longer, she knew that an opening would turn up.

She set her glass down on the coffee table, snapped open a fortune cookie, and began to nibble at it while stepping to the door that opened onto the upstairs porch. She could hear the traffic on Kapahulu Avenue and see the bright green sweep of a golf course to the west. Less than fifty feet away were the beautifully landscaped condominiums that Debbie had written about.

''Look at it this way,'' Debbie suggested. ''If

you can't get a hospital job here, just have a good vacation, then go back to Oklahoma City and find a position."

"I guess you're right." Sylvie didn't want to go back to Oklahoma or anywhere else. Hawaii was too lovely. She glanced at the narrow slip of paper from her fortune cookie. "Debbie, listen to this! 'Two's enough, three too many.' See, I'm not supposed to go back! Mom and George were set against my coming here with the money they gave me for graduation. I know what they hoped I'd use it for." She stood there for a moment, the flaming sunset behind her creating a halo around her light hair, then she returned to the rocking chair.

"A present is a present. How do you know what they wanted?"

"Mom and George have just been married two months, and I could tell I was in the way. It was said tactfully, but the money was supposed to help me set up my own apartment. George even offered to cosign with me." Sylvie took another fortune cookie from the basket. "Look—'Beware the pretty penny.' That's the thousand dollars they gave me."

"But you didn't even have a job. How could you have moved into an apartment and lived very long on that, especially if you had to buy a car?"

"They didn't expect me to. They knew I could get a job there easily. The *Sunday Oklahoman* always had ads. And George offered to drive to work downtown with Mom so I could borrow his car at first."

Debbie's eyes probed Sylvie's. "You really did want to come to Hawaii, didn't you? I thought I read between the lines that you wanted to get away from Fred Barton for a while, too."

Why did Debbie have to ask her about Fred

now? It was just one more thing to worry about. Before she decided to spend the rest of her life with one special person, shouldn't she be certain he was the right one?

Her mother had always told her that romance soon wore off in marriage and to be practical in choosing a husband. But things were different now. Thinking of George with his silly jokes, Sylvie couldn't help smiling. George didn't seem like much of a catch to her, but shouldn't she feel about Fred the way her mother obviously felt about George?

Debbie said softly, "Being here will give you a chance to decide, deep down. If you need to break it off with Fred, you'll find the courage to do it, and you'll give him a chance to find someone else. He's special, and he deserves a woman who really loves him."

Sylvie stopped her restless rocking and stared at her roommate. "You're right. I haven't been fair, letting him spend his time and money on me without making a real commitment to him. Maybe what I want in a relationship doesn't exist. Maybe I just don't know how to really love a man."

Debbie giggled. "Sweet, innocent Syl. When you're really in love, you'll know, and you'll be glad you waited. Love isn't something you can define. If good looks were the key, you'd have married Fred by now, school or no school. He's terrific-looking, you know—so tall and broad-shouldered and strong. Remember how we used to watch him play football?"

"Talking about Fred, I just realized that I've been so busy, I haven't written to him once since I got here."

Debbie jumped up and ran her fingers through her short, curly brown hair. "Enough heavy talk now! You've had a rough day. I'll treat you to dinner in a Japanese restaurant I know. How about it?"

"Are you kidding? Let's go! Maybe tomorrow I'll find the perfect job and everything'll be fine. But one thing is for sure—I'm going to stay here for a while, somehow."

Debbie guided her little blue car expertly through the evening traffic, skirting Waikiki Beach with its phalanx of tall, modern hotels and hordes of tourists. "I see the *malihinis* are out in force," Debbie said, waving toward the milling crowds.

"The what?" asked Sylvie.

"*Malihinis*—tourists, newcomers."

As Sylvie commented, "Look, everyone seems to be wearing a lei," a grinning young man roared up beside them on a Honda motorcycle.

"Hi, missy," he called. "You need another lesson? I teach you tomorrow."

"Who on earth was that?" Debbie asked.

"Sam Something-or-other," Sylvie replied. "He was on the beach at Waikiki the day I got here. He said he'd teach me to surf cheaper than they would at the regular concessions, so I took two lessons from him. He made it so easy. There's really nothing to it."

"I should've warned you about those fellows," Debbie said. "They're all over the place and they can spot a new prospect a mile away."

His long black hair and his unbuttoned shirt flying in the wind, he waved as he zoomed by. The blast of his motorcycle soon was lost in the cacophony of automobile horns, with Hawaiian melodies and pounding rock beats emanating from the souvenir shops and bars.

"This is like the midway at the state fair," Sylvie shouted above it all. "Where are the quiet, romantic beaches I've heard about?"

"Give it time. You'll find your own special

beach and it'll hold whatever you want it to,"
Debbie said, her serious glance at Sylvie belying
her bantering tone.

"Right now I'll settle for dinner. I'm starved.
Where are we going?"

"You'll see." Debbie parked and led Sylvie
into a bustling restaurant filled with laughter
and recorded Oriental music. "Behold, The
Hibachi House, where you can prepare your own
poison," she said with a flourish. "I like it because it's cheap and good. I just wish everyone
else didn't like it so much too. But the food is
worth putting up with the close quarters."

Soon they were seated at a griddle-top table,
grilling thin strips of beef, water chestnuts, bean
sprouts, and mushrooms, then dipping them
into tiny bowls of various sauces.

Swift waiters, who seemed never to stop
smiling, bowed and took care of the continual
flow of new customers. "They keep finding
space for one more," Sylvie remarked, when a
portly man at the next table stood to leave and
bumped her elbow, then apologized profusely.

"This is like one big party, isn't it? I knew
you'd like it." Debbie turned her meat with a
long fork and glanced around the room. "My,
my, see who's slumming," she said under her
breath, watching a slender woman of about
thirty-five push her way past the man who had
just left and take the seat he had vacated. Her
green silk dress shone in the light from the wall
torchères, and her wedge-cut dark hair framed
an ivory face that looked as if it rarely smiled.
She wore carved jade earrings and several gold
chains around her neck.

"Hello, Virginia," Debbie said, raising her
voice over the hubbub. "I see you didn't feel like
cooking either. Not that this isn't cooking, but at
least there's no cleanup afterward."

Her eyes fixed on her menu, the woman replied, "I don't cook. It's a waste of time, and so is idle conversation."

Ignoring the rebuff, Debbie continued, "Virginia, this is my new roommate, Sylvie Brooke. Syl, Dr. Virginia Gamble."

Virginia acknowledged the introduction with a glance and a nod.

Meeting expressionless steel-gray eyes fringed by sooty lashes, Sylvie asked politely, "Do you work at the same hospital as Debbie?"

"No, I do not," she replied flatly, making Sylvie feel that she had somehow insulted her. "I'm a marine biologist, not a physician." She then returned to her menu.

"How interesting," Sylvie remarked. "This is the ideal place to be a marine biologist, since we're surrounded by the ocean."

"Quite. And now, if you don't mind, I need to order."

Sylvie flashed a wry glance at Debbie. Debbie smiled at her and said, "Virginia, Sylvie just moved here last week. She's trying to find a job."

"You mean she's come to swell the ranks of the unemployed, don't you? This used to be a paradise, but what with all these tourists and the unskilled job seekers, it's getting to be something else altogether. There aren't many of us who really belong here." She cast a disdainful glance around the congested restaurant. "Miss Brooke, you'll find it takes more than a pretty face to get a job." She then turned and summoned a waiter.

"Come off it, Virginia," Debbie countered after the older woman had ordered. "Syl isn't unskilled, and she's too nice to realize she's just been insulted. In fact, she's a medical technologist, like me. I was a year ahead of her in school, and that's why you're so lucky as to have known me longer.''

Debbie's grin drew a grudging smile from Virginia, who said, "Call it luck or call it something else. You're one of a kind, I must admit. And as for you, Miss Brooke . . .''

"Please, call me Sylvie.''

"As you like, Sylvie. Do you have any experience other than your schooling?''

"No,'' Sylvie conceded, looking away. This woman, whom she barely knew, had a gift for making her feel extremely uncomfortable.

"There, there, our feelings are hurt!'' Virginia's laughter held a cutting undertone.

"That's enough,'' Debbie intervened. "Syl doesn't realize you're nasty most of the time and your insults aren't for her personally, but just part of your generally unpleasant disposition.'' Debbie's smile negated her words.

Virginia made no response. Having finished her dinner, she lit a cigarette, inhaled deeply, and, with her chin tilted and her eyes half closed, asked, "Do you have any references, Sylvie?''

"*I'm* her reference,'' Debbie shot back.

"Oh, you! You'd give a reference to a two-headed chimpanzee if you thought it needed help.''

"I knew Syl at college for three years and then we trained together at the university hospital for three months,'' Debbie replied calmly. "But you can call the department head and check.'' She wrote a name on a napkin and handed it to Virginia.

Sylvie shifted uncomfortably in her chair. She was beginning to feel confused. Was Virginia considering offering her a job? Biology had been her major, but marine biology was a specialty she knew little about.

Virginia volunteered, "I'm the director of the Wai Huihui Seafood Plantation and I've been thinking about asking our head office for an assistant. My work load gets heavier all the time." She narrowed her eyes and watched the smoke from her cigarette drift toward the ceiling. "If I found someone suitable myself, I'd have a better chance of getting approval. Less red tape."

Sylvie tried to conceal her growing excitement. This wasn't the sort of job she had imagined, but if the salary . . .

"Come on, girl, wake up! Are you interested or not?"

"Yes, Dr. Gamble. Of course I'm interested." She stopped to collect her thoughts. What she said now might be crucial. "I'd like to be considered for the position. I'd love to stay in Hawaii, but right now there are no med-tech openings in the local hospitals."

"If all you want is an interim job," Virginia snapped, "forget it. I'm far too busy to waste my time training you if you're going to quit as soon as you find an opening at a hospital."

"I didn't say I'd do that. I'm not a job hopper. I worked at the same department store during vacations from the time I was sixteen." Sylvie fought an instinctive antagonism toward Virginia. She knew it would be difficult to work with her, but she could try. She needed the job. As an assistant, perhaps she would be doing detailed procedures and not working side by side with this woman. Marine biology might even prove fascinating.

"Well?" Virginia asked impatiently. "What's your answer?"

"I was just thinking how interesting the field sounds. I'd like to hear more about it."

"For starters, the salary probably will be in

the vicinity of twelve thousand a year. I'll let you know definitely after I talk to the head office."

"But I could—" Sylvie bit her lip. She could earn more in her own field, but there were no openings now. "That's not quite what I anticipated, but if you're satisfied with my performance, I'd expect a sizable raise within a few months."

"So, you're one of the quietly assertive ones!" Virginia laughed. "What would you consider a sizable raise?"

"I know I can start at fifteen thousand in any hospital." Sylvie did not feel nearly as confident as she managed to sound.

"And just how many offers have you had from hospitals?" Virginia was the cat, Sylvie the mouse.

"Come on, you two," Debbie interrupted, turning from one to the other. "Virginia, you need an assistant. Syl, you need a job, and I'm sure Virginia can do something about the money. She's the boss."

"Just the director of the place, but I do have influence with the owner. I'll try to get you a little better starting salary, and if you work out, you should be making what you want within a year. How does that sound?"

"Fine." Sylvie smiled. "Here I'm accepting a job and I don't even know what a seafood plantation is or what my duties will be."

"Your duties will be to assist me in any way I tell you. You won't be doing anything I haven't done myself hundreds of times. You'll see what a seafood plantation is when you report for work. We raise oysters."

"For pearls?" Sylvie pictured mounds of lustrous gems. This indeed was exotic Hawaii.

"No, no, no. Sea*food*, just as the name says.

Don't worry, you won't have to open them or
can them. We have laborers for that. The plant
is completely automated, and the temperature,
pH, and so on have to be monitored. Then, of
course, we grow plankton to feed to the oysters.
It's really quite a complex operation, but I'm
sure you'll learn with my guidance."

"I'll do my best," Sylvie said brightly, her
head awhirl with thoughts of oysters, nimble-
fingered Hawaiian laborers, and automated pH.

Virginia handed her a business card. "Call me
in a couple of days and I'll tell you if and when
you can start. In the meantime, I'll check your
references." She looked at her watch, then left
without saying good-bye.

"I hope I get the job," Sylvie said, looking after
the retreating figure.

"Don't worry," Debbie assured her. "With
your excellent references, the job's in the bag.
Are you happy?"

"*Excited*'s more like it, but a little worried
too."

"You don't have to worry about Virginia. I've
known her casually for six months or so, and
she's always like that, except when there are
men around. Then she's all charm." With a syn-
thetic smile, Debbie picked up the squat blue-
and-white china teapot from the table. "Dear
Steve," she simpered, "do let sweet little me
pour you some of this perfectly precious hot tea
I've brewed just for you." Batting her eyelashes
and using exaggerated motions, she filled her
and Sylvie's tiny Japanese cups.

Sylvie laughed. She cradled her cup in her
palms and sipped the tea. After her long, tiring
day and the demanding encounter with Virginia,
she liked the soothing effect of the aromatic
steam surrounding her face. "Speaking of men, I

ran into the best-looking one today. He was so handsome, I had the feeling he must've escaped from a movie set."

"My, oh my!" Debbie feigned disbelief. "Where did you meet him?"

"I told you, I ran into him. Literally. Face first!" Sylvie laughed. "But he got angry because I wasn't looking where I was going. My purse fell and my billfold landed on the bed of a pickup truck. He ran downstairs and chased the truck, and that made him too late to go to the employment agency I'd just come out of." She smiled shyly, thinking of his startlingly bright blue-green eyes.

"Never mind, if he didn't have a job and was that pretty, you wouldn't want him anyway. He's probably one of the beach boys you see on Waikiki with their surfboards, posturing for the rich women tourists. Like that Sam we met on the way over here. Only, of course, you aren't a rich tourist."

"I don't think he's one of those," Sylvie said earnestly. "I saw him get into a Jaguar. Besides, he didn't seem the type to be a gigolo. And he's too rugged-looking to be called pretty."

"From the way you describe him, I'd say he seems just the type," Debbie insisted. "But why was he going to an employment agency? A gigolo wouldn't be looking for a job that way!"

"Now you're teasing me! But it doesn't matter, I'll never see him again and I really don't care. He was almost as nasty as Virginia, and two of those in one day are two too many."

"He did save your billfold, and Virginia did practically offer you a job, so don't be too hard on them. And speaking of jobs, we'd better head home. It's ten o'clock and I'm a working girl, like you'll probably be next week." Debbie paused for a moment. "You'd better call her Friday. If she says the word, she'll expect you to report to her on the double."

Kalakaua Avenue was a riot of bright lights as Debbie pulled out into the traffic. "Want to use the car tomorrow?" she asked. "I can call Mary Ruth early for a ride to work, and you can drive clear around the island if you want to. There's a beautiful scenic road and you can't get lost." By the time Debbie had finished telling Sylvie about the points of interest and how to find the seafood plantation in case she wanted to look it over, they were home.

Too excited to relinquish the eventful day, Sylvie tossed restlessly in her twin bed long after Debbie was asleep. Having almost found a job made all the difference in the world. Now she could relax and enjoy this tropical wonderland. Tomorrow she'd borrow Debbie's surfboard and find a secluded beach where she could practice what Sam had taught her at Waikiki. She was a good swimmer. The last time she'd ridden the board in, she'd been able to stand up with perfect balance all the way, knowing the thrill of the spray in her face, with her hair blowing like a banner behind her.

Still too restless to sleep, Sylvie turned over and looked toward the window. The full moon shone through the sheer curtains and seemed almost to beckon her to the little upstairs porch, where perfume from unseen blossoms wafted through the air. The grounds below, silvered by moonlight, had a palpable air of unreality which made Sylvie feel unreal too. Who was Sylvie Brooke, and why was she here in Honolulu, so far from home?

As if searching for an answer, for her future, she looked out into the soft night. On the lanai of the closest neighboring condominium, two figures were silhouetted against the sliding glass doors. The tall, slender woman's proud carriage looked familiar, and, observing intently, Sylvie caught a glimpse of shimmering green. So that was how Debbie happened to know Virginia. They were neighbors.

Watching the couple was as bad as eavesdropping, but Sylvie was fascinated by the sound of Virginia's throaty laughter, its provocative resonance so different from her clipped, strident tones at the Japanese restaurant. The man, whose back was toward Sylvie, sat down at a table and Virginia poured him a drink from a crystal decanter. He stood up, then, and turned to look at the moon.

Sylvie stifled an exclamation. There was the stranger who had rescued her billfold—the most handsome man she had ever seen—and he was with that woman. But what difference did it make, after all? With their unpleasant dispositions, they made a good pair. Ignoring an unreasonable twinge of disappointment, she backed inside and looked out through the open door. She didn't want either of them to see her. Virginia put her hand on his arm and together they walked into the house. Sylvie hurried away. She would not stand there and watch the lights go out. Her bare feet padded over the tatami mat as she felt her way back to her bed. She tried not to think of the rendezvous she had just witnessed, and, after a while, visions of the rhythmic waves she would ride tomorrow lulled her to sleep.

Two

Sunlight warmed Sylvie's face as she lay listening to the chirping of the sparrow that had awakened her. She'd overslept! She'd be late for class! Then she sat up, opened her eyes, and laughed. She'd thought she was back in her own bedroom at home. How long would it take for her to remember upon awakening that she was here in the Hawaiian Islands, thousands of miles from Oklahoma?

Debbie must have crept around quietly and left for work. Her sheets were rumpled and the clothes she had worn the night before were piled on the tatami mat beside her bed. Neatness wasn't one of Debbie's virtues. She kept too busy moving on to the next adventure to pick up after the last. That was one reason why she was so much fun. Something new always happened with Debbie around.

Sylvie bounced out of bed with a Christmas-morning kind of anticipation. Life's gift to her right now was an entire day to herself for explor-

26

ing, surfing, answering to no one. She might drive all the way around Oahu on the coast road, as Debbie had suggested last night, or find a secluded beach and surf to the point of exhaustion, then nap on smooth sands in glittering sunshine. She might even try to locate the Wai Huihui Seafood Plantation so she would know where to go to work on her first day, if Dr. Gamble got permission to hire her.

That was the cause of her elation—the knowledge that for the first time in her life, she could control her future instead of having to live up to someone else's expectations. She was free of her mother's concerns, her professors' demands, and Fred's—what? His claim on the rest of her life. Fred wanted her to be sure, and he would wait patiently for her decision. But she had decisions to make too—whether to make a career of hospital work, or stay with the seafood plantation, or marry Fred. But not today! Today was strictly for adventure and pleasure.

Debbie had left her two slices of sweet, fresh pineapple, which Sylvie ate for breakfast with raisin toast and milk. After a quick shower, she made the beds and styled her thick blond hair into a long plait that would keep it out of her face while she was swimming. With her scarlet bathing suit under a pair of white shorts and a gauzy flowered cover-up, she slipped into her thongs and headed down to get Debbie's surfboard from the ground-level storage area of the carriage house. After struggling to get the half-size board out of the storage area and over to the car, she realized that it was too long to fit in the back seat of the Monza. Then it occurred to her to push the board in through the hatchback and lean the passenger seat forward to make room. Smiling with pleasure at her ingenuity, she climbed into the car and studied the map Debbie had marked for her with directions to the sea-food plantation.

There were two ways to go. Although the more scenic route was a little longer, Debbie had said it was worth the extra driving. That was good enough for Sylvie. She could think about distances later, when she had to get to work on time. And she would have to look for a used car soon, for she didn't want to be tied to a bus schedule.

Sylvie headed toward the wedge-shaped profile of Diamond Head, Honolulu's famous landmark. Rounding the craggy profile of the mountain on Diamond Head Road, with the extinct volcano on her left and the blue ocean with white-crested waves on her right, Sylvie felt almost as if she were driving along in one of the picture postcards Debbie had sent her. She had seen Diamond Head on TV and in photographs so often that being here gave her a feeling of déjà vu.

Palms and oddly twisted pine trees grew close to the beaches she passed, and there were flowers everywhere. She followed tree-shaded Kahala Avenue beside the hibiscus borders of the Waialae Country Club links. She slowed down to consult her map when she passed between Koko Crater towering on the left and Koko Head on the seaward side. Mrs. Means, Debbie's landlady, had told Sylvie that, according to legend, Koko Head and Koko Crater had resulted from the goddess Pele's last attempts to make a home for herself on the island of Oahu, before giving up and moving to the island of Hawaii, where she still made herself known through the eruptions of the active volcanoes.

Debbie had said Sylvie must be sure not to drive past Koko Head without stopping to see Hanauma Bay. Leaving the highway, she drove to the parking area, then walked down the steep, winding trail to the beach, where she found an elderly man photographing his small, sun-burned wife against the breathtaking back-ground.

"Would you like for me to take one of you to-gether?" Sylvie offered.

"Thank you kindly, young lady," he said. He adjusted his Leica and showed Sylvie where to stand, then joined his wife, whose blue polyester pantsuit rivaled the brightness of the ocean. "Now I'll take one of you, to return the favor, and we can send it to you when it's developed," he said. Sylvie gave him Debbie's address.

During all of this he maintained a running commentary, explaining to Sylvie and his wife that the bay used to be a crater, one of several on Oahu that were formed during the island's last volcanic eruption, some ten thousand years ago.

"Was that when Pele was trying to make her-self a home?" Sylvie asked.

The man consulted his guidebook, then shook his head. "It doesn't mention Pele, but it says the weathering of nature opened this bay to the ocean, and then they blasted channels out to its coral bottom for snorkeling and swimming." He put the guidebook back into his camera bag and asked his wife, "Want to stay here and take a moonlight swim tonight, honey?" He pecked her cheek, then winked at Sylvie. "We're here all the way from Iowa to celebrate our golden wedding anniversary."

"Now, Charlie," said the round little woman, touching her cheek where he had kissed it. Then she tucked her hand into his and smiled up at him, her eyes alight with a devotion that made Sylvie think of Mom and George.

In the bay, several bronzed young men were snorkeling. Sunbathers lay in groups on the beach, and a young couple, holding hands, followed a rocky trail off toward the eastern headland. Everyone seemed to belong with someone. Everyone but Sylvie.

The turquoise water of Hanauma Bay shaded to emerald green and amethyst in the channels, creating a rainbow effect. Out beyond the reefs, the sea was a deep, iridescent blue. To the west, Koko Head formed a backdrop for the curve of the palm-fringed bay and the glorious morning sky. *I want to stay here forever*, she thought; then, unbidden, came the thought: *but not alone. And—not with Fred?* She snapped a door shut on that thought, waved to the elderly couple, and rushed back up the path. She drove off with a squeal of tires. She wasn't lonely! She was free!

After she noticed the Kakapuu Lighthouse on its black headland, she slowed the car to a crawl. The private road leading to the seafood plantation should appear any second. She jumped at the sound of an impatient horn as a white sports car swerved out from behind her and streaked past. As it disappeared around a curve, she recognized the streamlined silhouette of a Jaguar.

She almost missed the narrow turnoff on the right. Seeming little more than a driveway, and surrounded by overhanging tree branches and flowering shrubs, it was barely noticeable. After a short distance seaward, the narrow road curved abruptly and was spanned by a white metal arch that announced: WAI HUIHUI SEAFOOD PLANTATION. A smaller sign riveted to one of its supports at eye level warned: PRIVATE. NO TRESPASSING.

Sylvie parked the Monza off the road just outside the gateway into a jungle of ferns, then stood uncertainly by the open gate. It would be easy to slip into the private grounds and look around, but what if she should come upon Dr. Gamble? She didn't want to appear overly anxious. Many times a little thing like that could make the difference between being hired or not. Finally, she decided not to push her luck. Instead, she would explore the narrow little path that originated just inside the archway and angled sharply down toward the sea. From where she stood amid the dense tropical foliage, the waves seemed to call her with their rhythmic murmur.

Careful to keep her footing, and grabbing an occasional overhanging branch for support, she hurried downhill. Suddenly the vegetation opened, and below her was a tiny cove with a white sandy beach that curved gently toward an odd rock formation. The sand was punctuated by palms that leaned gracefully toward the water. Crested breakers hit the headland and sent spume skyward, while the rolling swells coming toward the beach appeared just the right size for Sylvie's modest surfing skills, and there was no one in sight to observe her beginner's form. The spot was perfect.

She retraced her steps back to the car, got the surfboard, and managed to get it down to the beach. Glad she had worn her swimsuit, she dropped her shorts and cover-up at the foot of a palm tree. Feeling hot and sticky after the exertion, she waded into the refreshing water, guiding the surfboard before her. When the water became deep enough, she swam and pushed the board ahead of her.

Finally she raised her head to estimate how far out she should go to pick up one of the swells rolling toward shore, and saw a man in a black swim trunks standing at the foot of the jagged headland on the right. He waved both arms and shouted something to her. Although she couldn't hear his words over the sound of the surf, she waved and returned his greeting.

He cupped his hands around his mouth and shouted again. Was he trying to tell her this was a private beach? Bringing the surfboard down the path had been a lot of trouble, and now that she had swum out this far, she was going to ride a wave in, no matter what. Then, even if the man came and chased her off the beach, her effort wouldn't have been wasted.

What had begun as an exhilarating swim was becoming harder now and Sylvie found herself tiring. The deep-green swells were more powerful than they had appeared from the beach. At last she was past the headland, ready for her ride to shore. Not looking at the man in the black trunks, she maneuvered the surfboard around and grasped its sides. Then she slid over the tail in a prone position, balancing her body on a point slightly behind the center of the board, the way Sam had taught her. Balance was the most important part of surfing, he had emphasized. Slowly she rose to her knees, then with her left foot just behind the center of the board and her right foot behind that, her knees bent for balance, she felt a surge of excitement as a wave took possession of the surfboard and started rushing toward shore.

In a wild burst of happiness, she rejoiced at being one with the sea and the sky. On went the wave, cresting into a mountain of green depths. She had it! She was achieving the balance, timing, and coordination; she had the freedom she had longed for when watching skilled surfers. The world was hers, and . . .

It happened so fast that she didn't have time to worry or even to think. Her right knee buckled under her, and, in a maelstrom of churning water, she fell off the surfboard. Water swirled all around her, above and below her, so that she felt like a piece of driftwood, unable to distinguish between the bottom of the sea and the breaking wave on the surface. Then came a shuddering blow on her head, a torrent of salty water choking her, and a dizzying vortex of darkness.

Ever so slowly, Sylvie drifted into awareness of the rough texture of a damp towel beneath her cheek. She was lying prone, with hot sand scratchy under her chest and legs, and powerful hands pushing hard against the back of her rib cage. Saltwater dribbled out of her mouth and nose onto the towel, and she began to cough, feeling that she was choking. Then the hands ceased their insistent thrusts, and Sylvie, still coughing, rose to her knees. Without looking up, she took the wet towel and wiped her face, then blew her nose. Her eyes and throat burned painfully. Amazed that she was still alive, she kept her eyes closed against bright sun. The back of her head ached as if someone had hit her with a baseball bat. She touched it tentatively.

"I tried to warn you this was a dangerous place for surfing," muttered an annoyed male voice. "Leave it to a beginner not to have any sense, and to ignore an obvious warning."

Sylvie turned to look at her rescuer, whose black eyebrows were creased in a frown over startling blue-green eyes. Abrasive as ever, yesterday's handsome stranger seemed to be haunting her. "How was I supposed to interpret that pantomime?" she sputtered, coughing again. She sat on the sand, its warmth beginning to dispel the chill of her body. Looking out to sea, she touched her head again.

"You don't even know enough to get away from the surfboard if you lose your balance," he said sharply. "If I hadn't been here, you'd be dead. Do you realize that? The board hit you right on the head and knocked you out cold. What a scatterbrain!"

"I'm sorry," she said in a small voice. "Thank you for saving me."

He stared at her with eyes that squinted in the sunlight. Then he exploded, "I don't believe it!"

"What don't you believe?" Sylvie frowned, wondering why he sounded so accusing.

"It's *you* again! First you lose your billfold, then you nearly lose your life. I didn't recognize you with that silly braid and spouting water like a whale. I'm beginning to feel as if I've been appointed your caretaker!"

"No one asked you to be!"

"Did you expect me to let you drown?" He stood up, looked toward the sea, and demanded, "Why don't you stick to Waikiki with the rest of the *malihinis*?"

"I don't happen to like Waikiki Beach, that's why. It's too crowded. And I'm not a *malihini*. I live here."

Suppressing a smile, he mimicked, "Oh, you don't like Waikiki. How about one of the less dangerous beaches on the Kalama shore or at Barbers Point? I hope you're not going to tell me you're an expert surfer, because then I'll know you're a liar as well as a rather reckless, foolish young lady."

"Really!" Sylvie, sitting on the sand, weak and exhausted, felt her face flush with annoyance. Rising, she scooped up her shorts and shirt, then headed toward the path. She felt angry at his arrogant manner, yet she realized that he had really saved her life. "Thanks for your help, sir," she called back over her shoulder. He was watching her. "I'll try to repay you sometime, if you're unlucky enough to see me again."

"I don't think you ought to be going anywhere

for a while. You had quite a nasty blow, you know." The edge was gone from his voice and he looked at her like a stern parent.

Sylvie stopped and leaned against the trunk of a palm tree. She was dizzier than she had realized. He was right. She should have made sure that this was a safe beach for a beginner. But it had looked so inviting, just made to order for someone who didn't want to appear ridiculous before more-experienced surfers.

He strode up to her and gently guided her to the edge of the palm grove. "Come and lie down until you feel better. Did you drive, or do you live nearby?"

"I drove." Sylvie sat on the sand.

"You won't want to go out on the highway yet. Actually, you shouldn't be driving at all. I guess I'll have to take you home."

His manner made it clear that this would be an imposition, and Sylvie replied immediately, "No. Thank you, but I have my girl friend's car and she'll need it tomorrow. Besides, I'm starting to feel better."

He took his towel, rinsed it in the sea, and wrung it dry. Sylvie watched as he threw his head back to push a shock of dark hair from his forehead, then moved toward her, the muscles taut in his long, bronzed legs. "Here," he said, folding the towel and making a pillow of it on the sand, "lie down and relax for a little while."

She lay back, looking at the clear blue sky through fronds of the palm tree overhead. Blue sky, blue-green eyes . . . She looked over at him, wishing he were as kind as he was handsome.

As if reading her thoughts, he said, "I'm sorry if I was nasty to you. But for a minute there I didn't know if you were going to be all right or not. I felt responsible because I'd seen you swim out, and I was afraid. . . ." He was silent while his eyes followed the yellow and orange striped sail of a catamaran just rounding the headland and heading out to sea. "In surfing, if you lose your balance, you have to remember to dive as deeply as you can, right into the center of the swell, and you'll come up on the back side where the water is calmer and not so high."

Sylvie's head was aching less sharply. Listening to him, she closed her eyes and relaxed, feeling secure in his nearness and in knowing that he was taking care of her for the moment. She didn't know whether it was five minutes or an hour later when she woke. He was watching her as he lay prone at her side, his head on his folded arms. Caught off guard, his face had an almost boyish look.

"How do you feel now?"

"Much better," she replied, stretching. She sat up and smiled tentatively. "We don't even know each other's names. I'm Sylvie Brooke."

He offered his hand. "Steve McCloud," he said. He laughed, and she noticed for the first time the attractive cleft in his chin. Somehow it fit in with the face, the hair, the eyes. "You're right, it was about time we introduced ourselves. Of course, we've hardly had a chance. Whenever our paths cross, it's some sort of emergency, isn't it?"

He was teasing her in a good-natured way. She wanted to make some witty, provocative reply, but what was the use? Judging by the scene on Virginia's lanai last night, he was fully occupied with her future boss.

"Why are you frowning? Do you feel all right?"

"Oh yes, I'm fine now. I should go home."

He nodded, but seemed reluctant to let her leave. While his eyes followed the catamaran that had become a bright speck in the distance, his voice held her. "You haven't lived here long, have you?"

Sylvie shook her head and murmured, "Only about a week."

"And you're not working?"

"No, but I'll start soon. Probably this Monday." Virginia had told her to call in a few days. That would be tomorrow. Then there was the weekend. She wished she could spend all of it just sitting here on the warm sand with this man, looking at him and hearing his teasing voice, but she knew it was a preposterous idea. He was far too handsome and sophisticated to have any interest in a young, naïve girl like her. But at least for now she had his undivided attention. For a moment she toyed with the idea of telling him that Virginia was going to be her employer, but some instinct warned her not to. Then suddenly she realized that he was talking. "I'm sorry, what did you say?"

"I asked whether you've seen the Big Island—Hawaii—yet."

"No, just Honolulu and a little of the rest of Oahu. The usual things. An outrigger canoe race, torch fishing . . ."

"You've discovered the *lama-lama* already? It's quite a spectacle, the kerosene torches reflected in the water and the fish being scooped on board."

"*Lama-lama*," she repeated softly. "Hawaiian is such a musical language, I want to learn more and more of it. Then I saw Iolani Palace and of course Kamehameha's state and—"

"I know, all the tourist attractions," he cut in abruptly, as if dismissing her with the rest of the *malihinis*.

"But I loved everything," she said defensively. "And the food—it's so different and so good. I never tasted such sweet pineapples, almost like tangy honey. They just aren't the same at home."

"They're picked green, or else they would rot in transit. That's why the ones you buy on the mainland don't have much flavor."

He looked out to sea, then glanced back at her. "Where is home?" he asked.

"Oklahoma City."

"Why did you come all this way?"

"My best friend lives here and . . ." she hesitated, then blurted out, "I wanted to think about my future."

As if to relieve her apparent embarrassment at the impulsive disclosure, he looked away. Then he said lightly, "I have a suggestion for your immediate future. Would you like to visit the island of Hawaii?"

"Of course! I plan to see all the islands. I just haven't had a chance yet. I've spent the last two days looking for a job."

"I have to fly to the Big Island tomorrow—would you like to come along?"

"I couldn't possibly, but thank you." Until she was positive that she had a job, she couldn't afford to spend her money island-hopping, and she certainly wasn't about to let him pay for her ticket.

"I'd bring you back the same day. I have to go to my parents' sugar plantation and I thought it would give you a chance to see how the Hawaiians live away from the usual tourist haunts."

Sylvie sifted the fine sand through her fingers and found a tiny, pale seashell. She studied its pink interior as if it were the only object she had seen in her entire life. Finally she murmured, "I can't afford the trip right now. Maybe later, after I've worked for a while."

His blue-green eyes warmed her like the heat

of the sun. "Afford the trip? What are you talking about? You'll be my guest."

"I couldn't possibly let you pay for my ticket," she replied stiffly.

His laughter was clear and infectious, ringing out over the cove and echoing from the headland. A vein pulsed in his tanned neck while he threw back his head. "Who said anything about a ticket? I pilot my own seaplane and I'm inviting you to be my guest."

"Thank you, but . . ." Much as she wanted to go, she felt extremely foolish now.

"But nothing. Don't worry, I'm a good pilot and I'll keep you safe."

"It's not that." To hide her embarrassment, she was being stubborn and foolish. She had no reason to decline the invitation, except perhaps if he were engaged to her future boss. But even if that was the case, he wasn't suggesting anything but a brief excursion. It wasn't as if he were asking for a date. Then again, if Virginia was seriously interested in him and jealous . . .

"You see, you have no good reason, unless you have other plans."

She shook her head. "I'd love to go," she said softly, knowing she should have accepted the offer more graciously.

"All right then, I'll pick you up at nine tomorrow morning and I'll have you back before midnight. It's all settled."

She gave him her address and phone number. If he noticed that she lived near Virginia, he gave no sign. He stood on the bright sand and watched her climb the hill. Just before she reached the part of the path that plunged into the luxuriant vegetation, she turned and looked back. He was running toward a striped yellow and white object far down the beach.

She had forgotten all about Debbie's surfboard, which had been carried ashore while the undertow had pulled her out to sea after she'd fallen off. She waited for him, watching him carry the heavy surfboard under his arm with no apparent effort.

"Thank you so much . . . for everything," Sylvie said.

He closed her car door and grinned. Leaning toward her, he said, "I'll see you tomorrow morning, then."

Three

The telephone was ringing inside the carriage house. Sylvie heard it through the open window as she slammed the car door and, her head throbbing with every step, hurried upstairs. But by the time she'd unlocked the door, the ringing had stopped. Had it been Steve, calling to cancel their trip to the Big Island tomorrow? Feeling both frustrated and disappointed, she headed for the bathroom. She needed to shower and get rid of the saltwater that had dried to a grainy film on her skin and turned her braid into a lank rope.

The phone summoned her again just as she was about to turn on the spray. Was he calling back? Thinking how ridiculous it was that a man she barely knew should affect her this way, she wrapped herself in a towel and, her breath trembling in her throat, answered on the third ring.

"Hi," said Debbie. "I really didn't expect you

to be home yet, but I'm on my break now. I tried to call you a few minutes ago, too."

Of course it hadn't been Steve. She'd left him less than an hour ago. "I just got here. I heard the phone before, but I couldn't get inside soon enough."

"I just wanted to let you know I won't be home for dinner. I forgot to tell you about the birthday party for one of the techs."

"Have fun." After her almost-fatal surfing accident, Sylvie didn't relish the prospect of being alone this evening. She needed to talk it all out, but that wasn't Debbie's responsibility. She said lightly, "I might wait up for you if you're not too late."

"No, don't do that. These parties can run on and on, and I wouldn't want to think I was keeping you up. Tomorrow's my day off, so I'll sleep late."

"I wanted to tell . . ."

Debbie, who hadn't noticed Sylvie's interruption, continued, "If you write to Fred tonight, tell him 'hi' for me."

"I wouldn't know what to say. He'll be expecting to hear how much I miss him and that I've decided to go back and get married. I'm not ready to write that, though I suppose it would upset me to think about his marrying anyone else."

"Don't make him wait too long, Syl. It's not fair. Why don't you write and tell him to fly out here for a long weekend? We could show him all around Honolulu and maybe even take one of those cheap flights to the other islands."

"I don't have to wait for that," Sylvie said. "I might as well tell you now, since we won't see each other at all in the morning. I've been invited to fly to the Big Island tomorrow! I'll tiptoe out and try not to wake you."

"Sylvie Brooke! Who on earth are you going with?" Debbie's voice sparkled with curiosity. "You don't know anyone here yet, except me. And Virginia, but I'm sure she's out of the question."

"You'll never guess. It's the handsome stranger from yesterday."

"The gigolo?"

"He's not like that at all, Deb. He's a real take-charge kind of person, but he can be nice when he tries. This is too good a chance to pass up, before I get involved with my new job."

"You don't have to stand up for him. I was just kidding. All I can say is, you sure work fast. You're coming back tomorrow night, aren't you?"

"Of course. I should be home by midnight, but don't worry if it's a little later."

"Don't lose your glass slipper!" Sylvie heard the familiar jangle of the timer clock in the background, and Debbie said, "I've got to go. Have a good time and behave yourself."

"Good-bye," Sylvie said to the empty line. She would behave herself all right. Steve had made it clear that he considered her a silly young girl, rather than an attractive woman. But somehow, remembering how she had seen him with Virginia on the moonlit lanai made her feel uncomfortable. There was no telling how serious that relationship was. But one thing was certain—she would not let rivalry interfere with her work.

Sylvie woke in the early-morning coolness to find that it had rained during the night. Outside in the sunlight, diamonds were dripping from the branches of the shower tree. Sylvie had learned that because of Hawaii's nearly perfect climate, most buildings didn't have heating or air-conditioning. To get warm, she hopped out of bed and did a few quick toe-touches. Debbie was sound asleep in the other twin bed.

It was almost eight o'clock and Sylvie had to dress for the day's excursion, then call the seafood plantation to find out about her job. She hoped the phone call was a mere formality. If Virginia had checked her references, the new job was secure. Her counselor and department head would give her good recommendations, as they would any top student.

Sylvie brushed her long gleaming hair. Today she would wear it straight down her back, the way Fred liked it. "It's a molten gold cascade," he had said once, his voice catching as he ran his fingers softly over the contours of her head and neck, as if he were stroking a precious treasure. That was the most—the only—poetic thing he had ever said to her.

Cascade or not, Sylvie's long hair got in her way at times, but she liked the sensation of its weight enveloping her shoulders, and she wasn't about to give it up.

Looking through her closet, she wondered whether she should dress to meet Steve's parents or go casual, in case he took her to a volcano, as she hoped he would. She decided on low-heeled walking shoes, designer jeans, and a light blue silk blouse. It was a Liz Clairborn original and had been very expensive, but she'd felt it was worth it because it was so feminine and flattering.

Remembering that she still had Debbie's car keys in her purse, she scribbled on the telephone scratch pad, "Went to Hawaii with Steve McCloud (he knows Virginia), see you tonight," and left Debbie's keys on top of the note.

With some trepidation, she dialed Virginia's

number. A young woman's melodious voice informed her that Dr. Gamble was unavailable.

"My name is Sylvie Brooke," she said quickly, beginning to worry. "I was supposed to—"

"Oh, yes, Miss Brooke. I'm Mahina, and Dr. Gamble left a message for you. She said you're to report to work on Monday at nine. She'll be here to orient you."

"That's great!" Sylvie exclaimed, sighing with relief.

It was all Sylvie could do to keep from waking Debbie and telling her the good news. She added in capital letters on the note she'd written, I'VE GOT THE JOB! Sylvie Brooke was on her way! Independence was now within her grasp. Whatever her duties turned out to be, she was determined to do a good job. Virginia and the owners of the seafood plantation, who had authorized Sylvie's hiring, would be glad she was there. More than that, they would be delighted!

Promptly at nine o'clock, she heard tires screeching to a stop on the driveway below. She scooped up her blue sweater and purse and, restraining her desire to run, sauntered down the steps, unaware of how lovely she looked, framed among the blue flowers of the jade vine, with the breeze softly blowing her golden hair and the morning sun lighting her face.

Steve opened the door of the Jaguar and smiled at her. "Good morning. I'm glad you've come prepared. You may need that sweater."

"Does that mean we're going to a volcano?" she asked eagerly. "I didn't mean to hint. Whatever you've planned will be fine. I just thought it might be chilly if we were very high."

"We'll see how our time goes," he promised. "I have business at the sugar mill, and then if it's not too late, I'll take you to visit the new home of the goddess Pele. Have you heard the story of how she left this island and moved to Hawaii?"

"Yes, and I was also reading in the paper just the other night that they think she's building another island east of Hawaii."

He smiled at her again. "If you like fireworks, we'll go to Kilauea instead of the black-sand beach. We won't have time for both."

As he spoke, he drove expertly through the morning traffic until they reached what appeared to be an inland harbor. They passed through an open gate, then entered a fenced enclosure where several hangars lined the water beside the piers. Sylvie saw seaplanes, sheltered within, rocking gently on the calm, protected water of the bay. A blond young man pulled a small motorboat alongside as soon as Steve guided Sylvie down the three steps to the edge of the water. The young man then ferried them to a blue and silver seaplane, where Steve helped her aboard and took the controls.

When they were airborne, with Honolulu and Waikiki Beach stretching beneath them, Steve asked, "How's your headache?"

"I didn't know I had one," she replied. "Oh, you mean from yesterday." With her fingertips she examined the back of her head. There was a knot where the surfboard had hit her and it was still a little tender. "I guess I had forgotten about the bump," she said.

"Well then, it must not hurt much."

Perhaps he had asked her along out of sympathy and was regretting having brought her, now that he knew her injury was of little consequence. Then she chided herself for her insecurity. She had been around handsome men before, but she'd never felt so insecure. Perhaps she felt at a disadvantage because the billfold and surfboard incidents had made her seem so helpless. She looked down at the ocean glittering below in the sunshine, with sailboats and motorboats dotting its white-crested waters as if flung by a profligate giant's hand. She wanted to say something clever, but being so close to him in the small plane made her feel edgy.

They flew over the dry side of Molokai and saw rainshowers pouring over the mountains. Suddenly the sun came out and three rainbows, at first barely visible, became brighter and brighter right under the seaplane.

"I'm giving you an aerial tour of the islands. Perhaps some day you'll see them all at close range. Each has a personality of its own. Molokai is known as the Friendly Isle. Years ago it was known as the Lonely Isle because there was a leper colony on Kalaupapa peninsula. See where the lighthouse is? That's the peninsula."

Beneath them, the islands lay like emeralds. White beaches, offshore rocks, mountains, cultivated fields, houses, and trees blended in a toylike landscape. Bits of clouds hung about the highest points of Maui, and the red soil of the islands provided a brilliant contrast to the green vegetation and the blue ocean. The clear air and bright sun made colors extraordinarily brilliant, and even in the distance everything seemed to stand out in sharp relief.

"That's it! There's Hawaii, the Big Island, the best part of our tour. Forget everything I've been telling you about the other islands if you want, but open your eyes and your heart to this one. It's where I grew up, and no matter how many times I return, I feel a sense of awe—as if I were Captain Cook discovering it all over again." The almost boyish excitement in his voice made her heart turn over.

"It's beautiful from the air. I can see why you love it."

Steve busied himself with instrument readings and radio communication with the Hilo control tower, ignoring her as if embarrassed to have revealed his feelings. Finally he said, "There's Mauna Kea, the state's highest peak. If you like skiing, you'll have to come this winter."

"I love it! But I didn't know it ever snowed in Hawaii."

"Of course, you can't compare it to skiing on the mainland, but it's just as much fun. Now look there—see that half-moon bay on the coastline? That's Hilo Bay, where we'll land."

He brought the seaplane down in a wide arc and soon they were taxiing across the calm water, spray flying behind them like twin tails of a silver comet. Steve left the seaplane in a hangar similar to those at Oahu, then guided Sylvie to a station wagon parked on the dock.

"This open shore area seems more like a park than a waterfront," she remarked as they drove away from the bay and headed uphill through the town.

"Yes, it's magnificent," he said. "But no one envies the way Hilo got its open waterfront. It's referred to around here as instant urban renewal."

"What happened?"

"A giant tidal wave hit Hilo in 1960," Steve explained. "As any schoolchild around here can tell you, it was caused by an underwater earthquake off the coast of Chile. When the wave arrived here, sixty-one people were killed and there was millions of dollars worth of damage. Fortunately, Hilo is built mostly on high ground, so the waterfront took the full blow in that wide strip along the shore."

"It sounds more like urban removal than urban renewal," Sylvie ventured.

"Yes, it's been so long ago, people can joke about it now."

"I didn't mean to sound callous. It must have been horrible."

"Actually, there shouldn't have been such a loss of life. The Seismic Sea-Wave Warning System advised the islanders of the danger. But you know how people are. When they heard that at South Point the wave was only two feet high, some of the curious decided to go down to the waterfront and see for themselves. They made just one mistake! By the time the wave hit Hilo, it was sixty-five feet high."

"How dreadful!"

"You can be sure no one on this island will ever make that mistake again. But so much for that now." He pointed to a road intersecting the highway. "That's the way to the sugar plantation, but first I want to show you Lava Tree State Park. It's just a few miles south, and I think you'll find it interesting."

"There's so much to see on all the islands, it would take a lifetime."

"You have most of your life before you," he said, smiling. "How old are you? Eighteen? You must just have graduated from high school!"

No wonder he seemed so condescending at times! She replied lightly, but with a secret feeling of pride, "I've a B.S. from Oklahoma U. and I'm a medical technologist. But today I'm just an appreciative tourist."

"That's why I'm taking you to see the lava trees. We'll just stop for a few minutes, then we'll go to my parents' house. After lunch I'll take care of my business, and then I'll drive you to Kilauea," he said, as he turned off the highway into the state park.

An eerie landscape of tall black cones sur-

rounded them, and Steve, brisk and impersonal
again, explained that the cones used to be trees.
They had been enveloped by a flow of molten
lava and had burned, and the lava had formed
hollow tubes around their charred trunks.

"Could we get out and look?" Sylvie asked.

"If you want to."

Sylvie touched the rough surface of one of the
black tubes and, standing on tiptoe, tried to peer
inside, but the lava tree was too tall for her.

Steve's hands spanned her waist as he lifted
her easily. Her back against his chest, Sylvie felt
the warmth of his body and his breath in her
hair. More aware of him than of the lava tree,
she looked inside the black cone. There, cap-
tured in the hardened lava, a pattern of tree bark
was visible. "Oh!" Her whisper could have been
for the ancient tree or for the man who held her
suspended in an intimate, timeless moment.

Suddenly, voices signaled the arrival of a
group of tourists with their cameras. Steve lowered Sylvie to the ground, took her elbow, and
said, "Shall we go? I'm hungry and lunch will be
ready for us at the house."

Sylvie, trying to hide her disappointment, hurried back to the station wagon. She thought of
his parents waiting at the sugar plantation.
What would they think of her? Nothing, probably. No doubt she was just one of a long parade
of girls he had escorted to the Big Island, lifted in
his arms to see the lava trees, and introduced to
his parents. The entire day might be a carefully
orchestrated routine he had performed again
and again.

"My parents are in Europe for the summer,"
he remarked. He seemed to have a knack for
reading her thoughts. "I'm sorry you won't get
to meet them. They're special people," he said,

turning at the intersection he had pointed out before.

Soon they were driving between walls of sugar cane as tall as one-story houses. Farther on, a waist-high, blooming expanse opened on one side of the road and several acres of pink flowers rippled in the offshore breeze. Women wearing loose, brightly colored dresses and straw hats moved through the fields, picking the blossoms and placing them in tall baskets hanging from their shoulders.

"What beautiful flowers. What are they?"

"Vanda orchids. Did you know Hawaii is also called the Orchid Island?"

"Of course! I should have remembered that."

"Then you wouldn't need me," he teased. "You may have heard that Hilo boasts of being the orchid capital of the world. Millions of Hilo's blossoms are shipped to the other islands, Japan, and the mainland. Ours is just a small operation. I suspect my father raises these orchids to humor my mother. Our main crop is sugar cane."

"Look!" Sylvie sat forward in her seat. "There's a big fire off to the west. Should we warn someone?"

He laughed. "They're just burning the west fields. That's how we harvest sugar cane. The fire burns off the dry leaves. The cane is still too green to burn. It's taken to the mill where it's processed immediately."

They drove past some fields of short cane and Steve explained that it was seed cane, stalks grown for a few months, then cut into eighteen-inch lengths and planted to produce the harvestable crops. Huge bulldozers were chewing their way through acres of cane, shearing the stalks off at the ground, then cranes dumped the great bundles of cane into giant haulers, which crawled toward the sugar mill in the distance.

"It's not what I expected at all." Sylvie had envisioned native workers singing as they wielded their machetes, but this was more like an efficient, motorized construction gang.

The road turned uphill and the fields beneath them were shielded from view by tall trees with feathery crimson flowers that lined the road. Noticing Sylvie's admiring glance, Steve explained, "Those flowers are the red lehuas. They blossom on ohia trees. It's Hawaii's official flower."

"I thought the red hibiscus was the state flower."

"That's not bad for a *malihini*," he said, grinning at her. "The hibiscus is the flower of the state of Hawaii, which includes all the islands. But the lehua is the flower of this island, Hawaii. There's a legend. Lehua, a princess, and Ohia, a commoner, fell in love. As in all good legends, they were forbidden to marry. A sympathetic god turned them into blossom and tree so they would never be parted. The legend says that it rains if you pick a lehua. The raindrops are the tears Lehua sheds when she's separated from her lover."

"How romantic. I like sad love stories."

"Why? Have you had a tragedy in your love life? Has some man broken your heart?"

"Nobody's broken by heart. In fact, he's waiting. . . ."

"Yes?"

"Nothing. Tell me about the hibiscus. I know the Hawaiian girls wear hibiscus blossoms in their hair. Isn't there something about which side they wear them on?"

He looked at her quizzically, as if agreeing to humor her and change the subject. "Yes, if a *wahine* wears a hibiscus—or any other flower, for that matter—behind her left ear, it means she's single and, you might say, looking. If she wears it behind her right ear, it means she's married or spoken for." He eased his foot off the accelerator on a curve. "Here we are," he said, braking before a two-story white mansion fronted by tall, slender columns that supported an upstairs veranda.

"It's lovely. But what's a Southern plantation house doing here? All it needs is some Spanish moss hanging from the trees!"

"One of my forebears brought his architecture along," Steve explained, laughing. "Ah, there's Sumio."

A slender young Japanese man in a white coat bowed as he greeted them at the door. Steve introduced Sylvie and asked that their lunch be served in the sunroom.

Sylvie followed Steve through a spacious front hall graced by an arching stairway. She stopped at the open doorway of the dining room and murmured, "What a lovely room." The sun filtered through sheer curtains and reflected against the pale lilac walls. The pinks and purples of the Aubusson carpet complemented the mahogany furniture, and the prisms of the crystal chandelier cast tiny rainbows on the walls. The room was suffused with quiet elegance.

"Yes," Steve agreed. "As a child, I felt as if I should whisper in there. Come now, you'll like the sunroom. It's less formal."

He led her to an intimate room at the back of the house. Walls of windows and sliding glass doors made the room seem an extension of the flagstone terrace outside. The white wicker table was set for two, with sterling silver, linen placemats, and delicate china.

"Sumio, you may serve lunch now," he said to

the Japanese houseman, who retreated toward the door. "Just a minute," he called. "Miss Brooke might like a glass of sherry."

"No, thank you. It's so early."

"All right, then," he dismissed Sumio.

The glass doors and louvered windows were open and the room was heady with perfume from the garden, while birds sang in the trees outside. Above the table, vines trailed from hanging baskets, enhancing the illusion that the room was part of the garden outside.

"You like it?" Steve asked.

Sylvie realized she was smiling. "It's lovely! How can you ever leave this place?"

"I always come back," he said, smiling in return.

Sumio reappeared and began serving them unobtrusively. The faint nutmeg essence of the clear broth seemed to increase Sylvie's appetite.

When the entree was served, she savored the complexity of flavors and said, "This is delicious. What is it?"

"Galantine of turkey, one of my favorite dishes. The cook always prepares it when I'm expected."

"My mother's a good cook, but I doubt she could make anything like this," Sylvie said.

Steve's blue-green eyes looked into hers, and, as usual, she couldn't tell whether his expression was one of amusement, or understanding, or condescension.

"I'm sure your father doesn't complain," he remarked.

"My father died years ago," Sylvie said quietly.

"Tell me about him," he said.

She chatted on. A sweet current seemed to be drawing her closer to him. She had misjudged him. He was kind and understanding in his attempt to put her at ease. How mistaken she'd been, during their first two encounters, to think he was arrogant and unfeeling. She barely noticed the progression of their meal through a tossed green salad and dessert of fresh papaya with a sweet cream sauce. Sumio came and went, noiseless as a shadow.

Sylvie wanted this luncheon to last forever. How surprising it was that she and Steve had been acquainted such a short time, yet they could sit relaxed and at ease, not needing to fill with words every bit of time in the bright afternoon.

She was about to tell him about her new job at the seafood plantation when he pushed his chair back and excused himself, saying, "I must take care of business at the mill so we'll have time to drive to Kilauea. Rest here or on the terrace, or walk around the gardens if you like."

Sylvie stepped out onto the terrace and wandered through a little gate partially hidden by a red-flowering hibiscus. Impulsively, she picked a blossom and tucked it behind her left ear. A manicured lawn sloped gently downhill, and she could see the ocean in the distance. Bordering the grassy slope in a riot of color were bougainvillea, flamingo flowers, and some graceful yellow trumpet-shaped blooms, all framed in a background of tall, slim trunks of palm trees. A few hundred yards from the mansion, partially hidden among the flowers and ferns, was a white cottage. A gnarled pine tree in front of it gave the impression of a Japanese dwelling. It looked inviting, and Sylvie strolled toward it.

"Aloha," a soft voice called. On the back porch of the cottage, sitting in a cane rocker, was an incredibly old woman dressed in a long, flower-sprigged beige dress. Her eyes were opaque, the color of slate, and her wrinkled face was one big

smile beneath her snowy hair, which was fash-
ioned in a bun on top of her head.

"Aloha," Sylvie replied.

"Come sit with me awhile, child."

With a shock, Sylvie, who was already sitting
on a step near the rocker, realized that the old
woman was blind. Her face shone with contentment and intelligence, and her teeth gleamed in
contrast to her dusky skin. There was something about her features that made Sylvie think
of the old native Hawaiians, as did the necklace
of oddly shaped green stones around her neck.

The rocker squeaked in soft counterpoint to
the chirping of birds and the rustle of the palm
fronds. Sylvie sat, contented, letting the sun
warm her face. "The view is beautiful here," she
remarked, then drew in her breath. How
thoughtless for her to have mentioned the view
when her elderly companion couldn't see it!

Sensing Sylvie's unspoken concern, the old
woman said gently, "Don't feel sad for me. Now
that I'm blind I see things I never could see before. Besides, I remember everything well. But
tell me about yourself. You're not *he Kanaka
wahine.* Definitely not an island girl. Did you
come on a tour and become separated from the
other *malihinis*?"

"No, I wasn't born here, but I'm not a tourist. I
came with Mr. McCloud, who lives up at the
house over there." Sylvie pointed, then with-
drew her hand in quick regret, but the old
woman paid no attention. She drew herself up in
her rocker, planted her feet firmly on the clean-
scrubbed boards of her porch, and leaned forward.

"Come here, child," she commanded.

Sylvie scooted across the porch and touched
the old woman's knee. The small, gnarled hands

were soft as butterflies alighting on her brows, nose, and lips, as they traced the contour of her delicate features and the length of her hair.

"This is like spun silk. It is blond, I know. The color of the breast feathers of the *aniaiau*." She felt the hibiscus blossom behind Sylvie's left ear and leaned back with a serene smile. "Master Steve brought you, then. Have you come to stay?"

"No. We're just here for the day. Do you know Steve?"

"Do I?" Her laughter was a rippling stream. "I was his nanny and his mother's nanny before his. I do indeed. I also know I'll see you again, child. But I cannot keep calling you that. My name is Iolani. What is yours?"

"Sylvie."

"Sylvie." She rolled the name on her tongue, on her lips. "It is musical, like your voice."

They chatted on in the sun till Sylvie felt she should return to the big house. Steve would be back any minute. She took Iolani's hand in hers and said, "I hope I'll see you again."

"You will, you will." Iolani reached up and hugged Sylvie. Then she took off her green necklace and slipped it over Sylvie's head.

"Oh, I can't accept this. It's so lovely, and I'm sure you treasure it."

Iolani gathered Sylvie's golden hair and swept it over the necklace. "Master Steve's grandmother gave it to me. I have had it ever since I was a young girl. It was to bring me the smile of good fortune and a good husband. And it did. But my time is almost over now, and I want you to have it."

Impulsively Sylvie took the hibiscus from her hair and placed it in the old woman's hands. "Thank you, Iolani."

Iolani chuckled as she caressed the red flower. "Soon you'll wear a blossom behind your right ear."

Sylvie blushed and didn't reply. She traced the irregular shape of a light green stone, smooth as if polished by years of being touched by other fingers. "Thank you again. I love the necklace. And I'll come to see you again, I promise."

She ran toward the McCloud mansion, her heart beating in anticipation of seeing Steve and going with him to the volcano.

Four

The temperature dropped as the road climbed toward Kilauea, and the station wagon was soon surrounded by the rain forest.

"I wish there were time to show you the black-sand beach, where hot lava shattered like glass when it made contact with the cold water of the ocean. Over the centuries, the endless action of the waves has ground it smooth as silk."

"Sand like that would be fun to run in bare-footed," Sylvie said.

He shot her an amused glance, then began talking about the rain forest they were driving through. Giant tree ferns were green lace under the shelter of the blooming ohias, and a tangle of wild growth overran the ground. Steve stopped at the side of the road to let Sylvie hear the periodic plops of moisture dripping from the roof of the forest to its spongy floor as if the air had condensed into raindrops. She shrugged into her sweater and he reached across the seat to help her.

"You weren't wearing that necklace this morning, were you?" he asked, easing the car back onto the pavement.

"No, your nanny gave it to me." She tried to discern his reaction to this bit of information, but he offered no clue.

He said merely, "I see," and drove silently for a time. Then he remarked, "Iolani must like you. That necklace has a special meaning to her."

Sylvie wondered if Steve knew of the special powers the old woman ascribed to the green stones. Iolani believed this necklace had helped her find the right man to marry. Did he think Sylvie was hoping it would help her in the same way? She ventured, "Did she tell you what kind of luck she thought it brought her?"

"Oh, yes," he said, grinning. "Don't you know Hawaiians thrive on legends and traditions? That necklace, for instance—it's a gift from the goddess Pele because it's made of olivine, a volcanic stone."

Sylvie had no doubt that the green stones were of volcanic origin. As for the rest, she thought he was teasing her.

They drove into Volcanoes National Park and along Crater Rim Drive, and Sylvie immediately noticed the strange odor of sulfurous steam escaping through the many fissures on the slopes of the mountain.

They stood together at the lookout rail on the rim of Kilauea Crater, a saucerlike depression several hundred feet deep and more than two miles across. In the middle was a fire pit called Halemaumau, the House of Everlasting Fire. But there was no fire today. Nothing but steam issued from it, and Sylvie felt vaguely disappointed.

Then suddenly, as if on cue, there began a

gushing, roaring sound, and after a few tentative sparks, an incandescent spray of red-hot lava spurted several hundred feet into the air.

"Madame Pele is greeting you," Steve said.

"Is it dangerous?" Sylvie asked, thinking of Mount St. Helens' devastating eruptions. Instinctively she moved closer to him. His hand on the rail was so near hers that she could feel its warmth.

"No, don't worry. It's only the steep, symmetrical cones that are likely to explode." He pointed up to an imposing mountaintop wreathed in clouds. "The gradually sloping types like this one are usually well behaved. Instead of exploding, they simply crack open and let the lava flow out. If there were any danger, we wouldn't be allowed here. Madame Pele has a reputation for being ill-tempered, but she rarely claims lives. What she delights in is spewing out fireworks like these, and sending lava flows toward the sea. She keeps making the Big Island bigger. Hawaii is the only state whose boundaries are still being extended—by lava flow."

"You know so much about this that you could be a guide and give lectures," Sylvie said, laughing. "Have you ever considered doing something like that?" Then she remembered his consternation at finding the employment agency closed only two days before. It was hard to reconcile his concern that day with his family's obvious wealth.

"That's not quite in my line, I'm afraid."

She wanted to ask what his line was, but if he wanted her to know, he'd tell her when he was ready to. She wouldn't press him. His hand on the rail was barely touching hers now, and she kept her own very still, more aware of his nearness than of the fiery spectacle she had longed to see.

Suddenly he asked, "Do you like living in Hawaii, or have you had time to decide yet?"

She wanted to tell him that she'd rather be here with him than anywhere else . . . But she couldn't say *that*—the altitude must be affecting her reason! She shivered and hugged her arms.

"Are you cold?" He put his arm around her shoulders.

"No, really, I'm all right." Yet she didn't move away from him. She glanced up and he looked down at her. Snug within the curve of his arm she trembled against him. Her lips parted of their own volition as he cupped her chin and kissed her softly. When she responded, he kissed her again, his lips warm and demanding. Her arms went around his neck and she closed her eyes, entering an incandescent whirlpool of unknown sensations.

"Look at the fireworks!" A child's excited voice, followed by the sound of running steps, rent their embrace. Sylvie and Steve sprang apart.

A group of tourists crowded along the lookout rail to view the display. Sylvie stared at the orange-red fountain as she tried to sort out her thoughts. What had possessed her to abandon herself like that? She had led the way, and her glance had practically begged for his kisses. They hardly knew each other. He was still an enigma to her, and whatever he thought of her now would be all wrong. She wasn't promiscuous, yet he had, in a manner of speaking, picked her up.

"Don't look so stricken. They didn't see us," he said, taking her hand in his to lead her away from the chattering tourists.

Sylvie nodded, her hand still and limp in his. What was there to say? Her response a moment before would bely any words she could dredge up now.

"Let's go. We'll have dinner at the Kona Coast Hotel, and it's a long drive there." He smiled quizzically. "I always keep my word, and I did promise to get you home by midnight."

She couldn't read his expression. What if he thought she'd be willing to stay overnight with him and the dinner at the hotel was just a polite way for him to begin the interlude? She pulled her hand away. The thing to do was to keep her distance, try to act as natural as possible, and keep the conversation impersonal.

She looked down at the glistening lava beds in the crater. "Could we go down there before we leave? That hardened lava looks as strange as a moonscape."

"Yes, of course, if you want." He sounded indifferent, as if by reclaiming her hand she had rejected him.

Sylvie hoped she hadn't hurt his feelings, but nevertheless it was a relief to know he wouldn't put any pressure on her.

They started their descent into Kilauea Crater. From above it had looked like a sea of overlapping petrified waves, but on closer inspection it proved to have every shape imaginable. Solidified lava had twisted into coiled ropes, hollow pipes, and designs suggesting artfully draped satin.

As Sylvie bent to pick up some brown lava filaments, the thin crust of a lava pipe gave beneath her and she lurched to regain her balance. This desolate spot was no place to fall and sprain an ankle.

"Are you all right?" Steve reached to steady her, his strong grasp like a brand on her arm.

"Oh, yes, just startled." Her voice was unsteady.

He kept his hand on her arm and they began the climb back to the rim of the crater. The warmth of his body, the pressure of his hand, and the subtle fragrance of his cologne were a lure that almost made her forget her recent resolve. He swung her around to face him, and, knowing he was going to kiss her again, she pushed him away and ran ahead without looking back. She felt that her will to resist would vanish completely if he so much as touched her lips again. She hurried to the station wagon and he followed without a word.

They left Kilauea and finally he broke the silence. "Are you tired?" She might as well have been a complete stranger to whom he was merely being polite.

"There's no excuse for it," she replied. "That was such a short hike down into the crater, but I'm exhausted."

"When we get to the hotel, I'll make arrangements for someone to fly the seaplane from Hilo and take the car back," he offered.

"You don't have to do that on my account." She didn't want him to know how relieved she felt. Flying directly from the Kona coast would get them back sooner and shorten their time alone.

"I'd rather," he said firmly, in the manner of one used to making decisions. "That'll let us enjoy a leisurely dinner, and we'll fly straight to Honolulu."

"Good, then my roommate won't worry about me."

"I told you, I'm a man of my word." More than that, he was a man of such magnetism that Sylvie was disturbed by his strong effect on her.

Steve chatted impersonally about the various sights along the way as they drove to the Kona coast. There were cattle ranches, sugar-cane fields, forests, and the ever-present ocean, way below the highway at first, then close at hand. They passed barren stretches of old and new lava flows, majestically solidified on their journey to the sea. Some areas of the Kona coast resembled nothing so much as the semidesert parts of Arizona.

A deepening sunset splashed the sky and the ocean with a blaze of red, gold, and cerise shading into lilac in a breathtaking display. The trees, the sea, the coast, the mountains, and the clouds seemed to sing a hymn of beauty to the heavens. Watching the focus of color shifting from one portion of the sky to another, Sylvie sighed and relaxed to enjoy the grandeur of her surroundings.

They turned toward the sea from the upper road, and with the green perfection of a golf course on either side of them, they saw the pools, terraces, and gleaming white expanse of the Kona Coast Hotel ahead.

"I'm almost sorry to come back to man-made things," Sylvie said. "This has been a day I'll always remember." She stopped and quickly looked at Steve, hoping he didn't think she meant to dredge up what had happened on Kilauea. But he was concentrating on the driving and his expression didn't change at all. Relieved, she continued in a bantering tone, "In a way, I hate to give up my freedom and start working on Monday."

"Where will you be working?"

"Just off that beach where you rescued me yesterday."

"*Where?*" She was puzzled by the harsh tone of his voice and by the cold frown he gave her.

"At the Wai Huihui Seafood Plantation. You may be familiar with it." Of course he would know of it! Virginia was the director there. On

Kilauea, responding to his kisses, she hadn't thought about Virginia. Now memories of the scene on the moonlit lanai came spinning back—Virginia snuggled up to Steve as they lingered to look at the stars; Virginia pouring him a drink from a crystal decanter; Virginia leading him into her house so late at night.

Steve's silence was like a steel door between them. His handsome face looked as if it had been carved in granite. Without a word, he parked, helped her out, and guided her to an outside terrace with a view of the rocky shore and sea below. A hostess seated them at a table for two.

Sylvie chided herself for having withheld the information from him. If she'd told him before that she was going to work with Virginia, he probably would never have invited her on this jaunt. She hadn't been honest, so she deserved his anger. His relationship with Virginia must be a serious one. But then, why had he kissed her on Kilauea? Perhaps he had just been carried away like she had and now he regretted it. Perhaps he feared she would tell Virginia about today's romantic interlude. But of course she had no intention of doing that, and she wanted to tell him so, but his frosty demeanor stopped her. In miserable silence, she waited for him to speak.

"Yes, I know the company," he said at last. "I own it." He picked up a menu and, shutting her out, scrutinized it before ordering for both of them.

A fog of dismay enveloped Sylvie, and although the evening was warm, she felt chilled as she had in the high altitude of the volcano. She should never have allowed him to kiss her, but it was too late now. What had happened could not be undone.

If she had known he was going to be her employer, she wouldn't have embarked on today's journey at all. Her mother had always said romance and career just didn't mix. Becoming romantically involved on the job could jeopardize both the career and the relationship. Had she not realized this already, one look at Steve's face would have told her.

His manner toward her had changed completely. There was no more lighthearted tenderness. He didn't watch her obliquely or reach for her hand. The sparks were gone from the ocean hue of his eyes. Now they were agate-cold and impenetrable. He was polite, and heartbreakingly distant. If she had wanted to put some distance between them, she had certainly succeeded. Would it be better to talk it out, or should they ignore it altogether? Sylvie didn't know what to do. The situation was beyond the scope of her experience.

Finally, he took the initiative. "I should have known," he said, each word like a lead weight, "when Dr. Gamble told me she had found 'a little blond girl from Oklahoma' to assist her. Please forgive what happened this afternoon. It wasn't appropriate, and I take full—"

"There's nothing to forgive. I . . ." Unable to swallow, she toyed with her omelet.

"Please, let me finish, Miss . . ." Surely he wasn't going to call her by her last name! "Sylvie. It won't happen again, so you have nothing to fear. Dr. Gamble said your credentials were excellent. We'll put today behind us and forget it, as if it hadn't happened."

Sylvie nodded and felt miserable. He spoke with authority. This was not a man who was courting her, this was her boss. He was ordering her to forget how her hand had felt cradled in his, and how she had responded to his kiss up there on the rim of Kilauea.

She could almost hear Madame Pele's laughter

in the surf's whisper on the volcanic rocks below the terrace. She must have been in this land of legends too long, for she found herself beginning to wonder whether things would have turned out differently if she had made the temperamental goddess an offering of berries and fish, as the ancient Hawaiians used to do. Perhaps she should be grateful that the goddess had not sprayed her with ashes and suffocated her with sulfurous gases as she had done to the Hawaiian army moving against King Kamehameha so many centuries before, capriciously preserving their footprints for all time in the cooled lava. Relating that story during the carefree drive up the mountain early this afternoon—a lifetime ago, it seemed now—Steve had said that supposedly the soldiers, in their haste, had forgotten their offering to Madame Pele and had paid for the oversight with their lives. But there at the volcano lookout today, Sylvie hadn't been concerned with the mythical Madame Pele, or soldiers, or berries. She'd cared only about his strong arms around her.

"What would you like for dessert?" he asked, interrupting her faraway thoughts.

"I couldn't possibly eat another bite."

"Nonsense. You haven't even finished your omelet, which was little enough to eat after all the hiking we did at that altitude."

We weren't hiking all the time, her heart reminded him. Then she blushed with embarrassment, her fingers nervously stroking the smooth, irregularly shaped stones of the necklace Iolani had given her. Iolani was mistaken. The spell of the green necklace was not for Sylvie and Steve.

And what about Fred? The thought of him was like a soft mohair shawl on a cool evening. She knew where she stood with Fred. Perhaps she didn't even deserve him anymore, now that she'd proved herself so flighty. At this moment, marrying Fred seemed comforting and attractive. What was she doing on this wild goose chase in the middle of the Pacific Ocean? She belonged back home, where she was known and loved. Yet, she yearned for the arms of the man who sat across from her—so near and so distant.

Steve signaled the waiter and ordered mangoes in champagne for her, then leaned back in his chair and sipped his coffee while she ate them. The mangoes were exquisite, juicy, and meltingly sweet, better than any peaches Sylvie had ever eaten, and the champagne gave them a tang.

To break the uncomfortable silence, she murmured, "These are delicious. I've never eaten such fruit."

"You have a Haden mango in your own yard. I saw it this morning. And this is the season for them. Some people come to the islands in June and July just for the fresh mangoes, you know."

No, she didn't know. She knew only how much she missed the easy companionship they'd had earlier in the day. "Is the mango where I live the same kind as this?" At least this was a safe, impersonal conversation.

"No, its flesh is a little fibrous, but it's still very good. You'll notice several growing on the grounds of Wai Huihui. Help yourself if you want to try one for lunch sometime. If anyone questions you, tell them I said it's all right."

There it was again, the invisible wall. He was the owner and she the employee, a new and low-level employee at that, with Virginia inserted between them. "When Dr. Gamble told me about my job, she said she's the director of the plantation," Sylvie said hesitantly. "Do you spend your time there too?"

He studied her face and frowned. Did he know she was worrying about being near him constantly in a work environment? "No, I don't. I'm there very seldom, but I live just half a mile away. I have my private research laboratory next to my home and I spend some time there. But usually I'm in downtown Honolulu, where our main offices are."

She must have looked puzzled, for he added, "There's more to our company than the seafood plantation, of course. That's only part of it, just like the research lab." He looked at her over the edge of his cup and sighed. When he continued, there was an edge of impatience in his voice. "There's the sugar plantation and mill, and the orchids—surely you remember seeing them! Then there are real estate holdings and the manufacturing laboratory. Now really, do you want a detailed inventory of McCloud Enterprises?"

"I didn't ask you anything!" Sylvie snapped. It wasn't necessary for him to condescend to her, and she resented it.

"The seafood plantation and the research lab are my pet projects," he said in a more gentle tone. "The rest is more or less under the direction of my father, at least where financial decisions are concerned." His eyes softened as he looked out toward the sea, where the moon dripped silver over the calm ocean. "The challenge of research is what puts a spark in my life. Whenever I get an idea and it develops to the point of feasibility, I patent it."

"What type of research is it? Research is my main field of interest."

"Is it? Then why do you want to work at the seafood plantation? That's about as far from research as you can get."

"Well, I really want to stay in Hawaii, and Dr. Gamble offered me the job. There doesn't seem to be an opening for me in a hospital just now. Do you do marine biology research?''

"No, I patent culture media for the medical field. When you bumped into me . . ." He cleared his throat and began again. "When we bumped into each other, I was going to see Elaine Dutton because my medical technician had just informed me she was pregnant and wouldn't be working much longer. I was going to ask Elaine to find someone good to replace her. When Dr. Gamble told me she wanted to hire a medical technologist to be her assistant, I thought to myself, *What a waste of talent!* But Virginia—Dr. Gamble—was insistent on hiring you, and she can be worse than Madame Pele when thwarted, so . . ." He watched her through half-closed eyelids, and she wondered if he was thinking of what had happened between them near Madame Pele's home, just as she was.

Wave on wave, her thoughts flowed to the accompaniment of the surf. Everything was mixed up, and she felt responsible for it all. If she hadn't made Steve miss getting into the employment agency before it closed, she would have found the research job she wanted, for Mrs. Dutton would have called her immediately about the opening in Steve's laboratory. There weren't many unemployed medical technologists available. Then, yesterday she might have been at the lab being interviewed instead of driving to Wai Huihui, going surfing where she didn't belong, and almost drowning. Steve wouldn't have rescued her and invited her to spend the day with him here, or kissed her . . . What good were those kisses to her, to him, to anyone? Because their mutual attraction had become so evident, there was no way she could work with him in the confines of a research laboratory. But that was immaterial anyway, since

Virginia too was in the picture. That Pele-tempered woman would spew fire if Steve tried to move Sylvie into his lab. As the director of one of his pet projects, Virginia would surely have priority over the desires of a new employee. Yes, Steve would do whatever would keep Virginia happy.

The word *happy* triggered a memory of the cozy scene on Virginia's lanai just two nights before, and again Sylvie reviewed the tangled skein of events that had led her away from research, the type of work she really wanted. Robert Frost's lines mocked her:

> Two roads diverged in a yellow wood,
> And sorry I could not travel both

It was done now—lab job, almost found and promptly lost.

With relief, she let herself be pulled back to the present by the sudden glare of spotlights trained on the water from the hotel terrace. Thousands of small fish, drawn by the lights like moths on a summer night, swarmed to the surface. "Look!" she cried.

"Yes, I know. This is one of the reasons I wanted to bring you here. Watch now, the show is just beginning."

The water churned and a manta ray, its wingspan as wide as an eagle's, prowled among the tiny fish, swallowing them like an enormous vacuum cleaner. A seemingly endless stream of minnow-size victims kept seeking the surface, only to be sucked up by the giant manta ray, which was soon joined by another, then another.

Sylvie watched in mesmerized horror. Finally she said, "I've always heard about the chain of life, with the big fish eating the little fish and some larger creature eating the big fish in turn.

But don't you think this is a cruel sport, just to provide entertainment for the diners while the little fish provide dinner for their enemies?"

"That's the way life is. Survival of the fittest."

"I know. But this makes me think of Christians being thrown to the lions to entertain the Romans."

"Really, Sylvie, how maudlin." His sarcastic words made her cheeks burn.

Momentarily forgetting that he was her employer now and she should be careful, Sylvie glared at him. He was heartless. He was one of the manta rays of this world, with no sympathy or understanding for the underlings. How could she have thought she cared for him? Let him and Virginia have each other! Two manta rays together.

Suddenly she thought of Fred again—kind, sweet Fred, who understood her. He wouldn't have brought her to see such a grisly display. But the more she thought about him, the farther away he seemed. She was committed to trying her wings here in this exotic world of lei and lava, rain forest and manta ray. For her own satisfaction, she must succeed at her new job. Then, if she chose, she could return to Fred with her head held high.

When Steve left to call for the seaplane, Sylvie relaxed in her chair with a sense of relief at being out of his disturbing presence for a while. There was the flight back to Honolulu still to get through, but she could pretend to be asleep for part of it.

Tomorrow she would give Debbie a casual account of today's events—with one omission—and Monday she'd begin the routine of her new job. Between dealing with the abrasive Virginia and the enigmatic Steve, she hoped her life wouldn't develop into a long round of stress and uncertainty. She would try to be smarter than the little fish.

Five

Their night flight was as silent as the stars around them, stars paled by moonlight just as Sylvie's joy had been dimmed by the day's events. Below, lights brighter than stars hugged Oahu's angular coast, multiplying in Honolulu and climbing the mountains like innumerable St. Elmo's fires on a ship adrift upon a midnight ocean.

He drove her home and left her in front of the carriage house. She watched his headlights disappear, then noticed a yellow Toyota parked next to Debbie's car, which meant that Debbie had company. The fragrant night taunted her with its loveliness while she dragged herself up the stairs. Everything was as she had left it this morning, but she herself was very, very different.

Debbie was alone, sitting on the fat floor cushion, painting her toenails with bright red polish. Before Sylvie could ask about the Toyota, her roommate inquired with uncharacteristic sarcasm, "How was your day with the Hawaiian Islands' most eligible bachelor?"

"Just fine, thank you. But I wish you'd told me he owns the seafood plantation," Sylvie snapped.

Debbie screwed the cap on the nail-polish bottle. "How was I to know that someone you described almost like a gigolo was *the* Stephen McCloud that Virginia's been after all this time?" Her voice harbored a definite chill.

"Well, I—"

"Fred called," Debbie interrupted.

"Did you tell him I was out with another man?"

"Of course not!" Debbie's usual lighthearted tone was absent. "Why would I want to worry him or hurt his feelings?" She hugged her knees and stared intently at Sylvie, who had collapsed into the bentwood rocker. "Syl, listen to me. You don't have a chance with Steve. Keep running around with him and you'll end up like Virginia—angry and bitter. Steve's a playboy. He'll use you and discard you, just like what you're doing with Fred."

Sylvie was puzzled by her friend's obvious bitterness. In all the time they had known each other, Debbie had never spoken to her so sharply. They'd had their disagreements, but never anything like this. She knelt on the cushion and put her arms around her roommate. "This isn't like you, Deb. Will you tell me what's really the matter?"

"Nothing's the matter," Debbie replied, pulling free from Sylvie's grasp.

"Oh, Debbie!" Sylvie's hurt showed in her face.

Debbie burst into tears. "I was so happy to hear Fred's voice, but I couldn't think of much to say because I didn't want to get you into trouble. You know how much I like him. I . . . I guess I'm envious that such a good man is in love with you and it looks as if he'll get nothing but a broken heart, while I . . ." Her sobs interrupted the torrent of words.

That was it! Debbie had always taken the role of wise-cracking pal with Fred, but she'd been in love with him all along but hadn't made a play for him because she was Sylvie's friend!

Sylvie sat there thinking about the situation. Steve affected her as Fred never had, and even after the way things had developed between them, she still wanted to stay in Hawaii and see Steve again. It made no sense, but she couldn't help it.

Too, she realized that Fred might be better off with Debbie, who very evidently loved him. But Fred was a strong individual with a will of his own, and even if Sylvie should want to, she couldn't simply hand him over to her roommate. Anyway, she wasn't ready to do that yet. She needed more time. But right now her best friend was sobbing, the one who usually had the glib quip and the ready smile.

"Oh, Deb, I didn't know you were in love with him," Sylvie said gently.

"I'm not! I'm not!" Debbie protested, as if trying to convince herself. "You're the one he loves."

"I know, and please believe me, I do appreciate him. I'm sorry if you think I've taken him for granted. But everything here is so exciting and beautiful—it's almost as if I've lost my senses since I came."

"Please, let's not talk about Fred any more right now." Debbie wiped her eyes and started over. "It's Steve I need to warn you about. Because I'm your friend, I wouldn't feel right if I didn't share what I know."

"He's nice, Deb, can't you understand that?"

"I must be crazy!" Debbie blurted. "If you're right about my being in love with Fred, I'd be better off if you dropped him and got involved with that rich playboy."

"He's not a playboy! And he's serious about his work, I can tell. Besides, he saved my life yesterday—I mean Thursday. It's way past midnight."

"He saved your life! How romantic!"

"That wasn't a figure of speech. He really did. I almost drowned while I was surfing."

"Oh, Syl!" Debbie listened in wide-eyed concern while Sylvie shared the details of the accident. Finally she said, "And I thought you were just trying to change the subject. He deserves credit for that, but please, listen to me. I have to make you realize you're in over your head where both Steve and Virginia are concerned. I can picture you losing your job, losing Fred, who truly loves you, and ending up empty-handed. There's no way Virginia'll let you have Steve. She's been after him too long and she's too determined."

"You're making a big thing out of nothing." Sylvie had trouble keeping her voice steady. "I know he owns Wai Huihui and I know about his relationship with Virginia. I saw them together the other night. Thanks for caring, but don't worry about me. Steve—Mr. McCloud—and I barely know each other. He showed me around the Big Island today, and that's all. He said he leaves the seafood plantation to Virginia, so I'll hardly ever see him. Now please, let's drop the subject."

Sylvie rose, hugged her friend, then wandered

out to the veranda. Insects were chirruping their night songs and a lone bird hinted of dawn.

"In case you're interested, Fred's going to call back," Debbie said, joining her. "Also, Lucille, one of the switchboard operators at the hospital, just got married and is moving to Vermont. She wants to sell her car."

"The yellow Toyota parked in the driveway?"

"Yes. I thought you might be interested. It's about seven years old, but I had Jimmy at the service station check it over, and he said it's in good shape."

"You're a good friend, Deb. How much does she want for it?"

"She hasn't set a price, but I know you two can work something out. She said she'll make you a good deal if you take it right away. You could drive it to work Monday and come by the hospital afterward to settle things with Lucille— if you like the car, that is."

Sylvie felt immensely relieved. Now she could get around on her own and not be dependent on Debbie or the bus.

When the phone rang, Debbie looked at her. "Go on, Syl, answer it. That'll be Fred."

Of course. It was almost four in the morning here, but that would make it eight o'clock in Oklahoma City, and Fred was an early riser, even on the weekends.

"I've been wondering what you're up to." His voice, with just a hint of a drawl, was like a bear hug enveloping her across the miles. "I hear you've been finding a job and exploring the islands."

"Fred, you just wouldn't believe how beautiful it is here. I've never seen so many flowers in bloom all at the same time. And doesn't a seafood plantation sound exotic?"

"You'd better not like your new job so much I'll have trouble luring you away from it when we get married," he said, but he didn't sound worried.

"I've no way of knowing—how much I'll like it, I mean. I don't start till Monday. Debbie told you about Wai Huihui, didn't she? Doesn't it sound fascinating?"

"No doubt." Irony didn't become Fred. Then he asked, "Have you thought about setting a date yet? You've been gone a long time already."

"Just a week." Here it was again, the pressure. "Fred, please stop pushing me. This is the first chance I've ever had to be my own person—to find out who I am and what I want out of life. If we're right for each other, then I'll have more to bring into our marriage. Can't you understand?"

"Well, I'm trying to. But I won't push you anymore. I won't even mention it again for a month, I promise."

Relieved, she chatted with him happily till she mentioned the yellow Toyota and he pointed out that it sounded as if Debbie was taking care of her now.

"If you're going to let her make your decisions, help you find a job, an apartment, even a car, it might just as well be me looking after you . . . and we'd be together." Although there was some truth in what he said, he wasn't entirely right. Debbie had been in Honolulu for a year and had a lot more contacts than Sylvie did. And Sylvie didn't have to buy the car if she didn't want it. That decision was hers.

"Fred, you promised! A month on my own, then we can start making plans or call it off," she reminded him.

There was a long silence, and the words—*call it off, call it off*—seemed to hum over the miles between them.

"I miss you, Sylvie. Will you at least write more often than you have been, which is zero?"

"Yes, I will."

He sent her a kiss over the telephone and Sylvie found herself retreating from the instrument. "Fred, it's nearly morning and I need some sleep. I'll write you tomorrow—today, that is—and again in a few days after I'm settled in my new job."

"I'll hold you to that. But I'd rather just hold you. How long are you going to make me wait?"

If he was trying to sway her toward the decision he wanted, he certainly was going about it the wrong way. He had promised and broken his promise twice already. "Good-bye, Fred," she said evenly.

"Okay, okay. Good luck in your job—I think. But don't enjoy it too much."

She hung up the phone, shaking her head. She needed to be free to concentrate on getting a good start at the seafood plantation, and she hoped the challenge of her new job would help her regain her perspective.

Monday morning was clear and sparkling, and Sylvie hummed as she took the shorter route to Wai Huihui that Debbie had shown her on Sunday, while Sylvie became accustomed to driving the Toyota and finding it a thrill to own her first car. She swung into the turnoff leading to the seafood plantation, ignoring the no-trespassing sign on the gateway since it didn't apply to her now. Less than a mile past the metal arch, the trees with their undergrowth of shrubs and ferns opened up, revealing a paved, airportlike expanse crowded with low concrete buildings. Men in overalls moved about with a purposeful air, and she stopped to ask one of them for directions.

He pointed to a tower of steel and glass that rose among a cluster of concrete tanks. The squat tower apparently was Virginia's aerie, from which she watched and directed the complex operation.

Sylvie climbed the outside metal stairway and knocked softly.

"Come in." Virginia sounded impatient.

"Good morning, Dr. Gamble," Sylvie said with a smile.

Virginia barely acknowledged her presence. She was busy inspecting a computer readout sheet.

From the windows of the control tower, Sylvie looked at the seafood plantation spread below her. There were several dozen concrete reservoirs filled with dark, tea-colored water. In the near distance were canvas-covered tanks and long trenches filled with water. A man on a tractor moved along one of the trenches, cutting some dark green limp vegetation from the water and moving it ahead toward nets at the end of the trenches, where it was hauled out and spread to dry.

"What is he doing?" Sylvie inquired when Virginia looked up.

Virginia looked out and replied, "Harvesting seaweed." She sipped coffee from a large blue mug as she propped her feet on her cluttered metal desk, then pointed to a coffeepot on a small table and invited Sylvie to have a cup.

"Let's get down to business now. I'll take you on a tour of the place so you'll know what the operation is like, but your main responsibility

will be with the plankton reservoirs. The pH—
that's the acidity balance—is monitored constantly, and the tanks have to be drained and refilled every four days."

Sylvie felt a small surge of confidence. At least
she knew that plankton were the tiny, almost
microscopic organisms that thrived in the
sea—that is, until they got eaten by larger fish.

Sylvie glanced at the maze below her again.
Was she to open a valve and let water flow out?
"You'll show me how to do that?"

Virginia frowned. "You don't do that with
your own hands. You instruct one of the workers. If there are power outages, an alarm'll go off
here." She pointed toward a computer panel.
"It'll be your responsibility to have the electri-
cian divert the auxiliary power supply to . . ."
She hesitated. "Until you learn your way
around, I'll have to show you. The power systems are of paramount importance. Right now
we're experimenting with raising two tanks of
European flat oysters; if we can keep them alive
and thriving, we have a Belgian buyer who'll
pay seventy-five cents apiece for them."

"How many oysters are there per tank?" Sylvie asked, looking down at the murky tanks below the tower.

"They're not in those, as you'll realize if you'll
just listen and stop interrupting!" Virginia
didn't bother to hide her impatience. "Those
tanks are the reservoirs where we grow the
plankton, which is what the oysters eat. Each
reservoir produces enough plankton to feed one
oyster tank. The oysters are over there." She indicated the canvas-roofed tanks lined up nearby.
"Those tanks under canvas are over a hundred
fifty feet long. We stack the oysters in each of
them in trays. The canvas keeps the sun from
boiling them alive, of course. You wouldn't be-

lieve how many oysters you're looking at right
now."

Sylvie was interested, but she didn't dare ask
any more naïve questions.

"See the two tanks marked with red numbers?
The ones closest to us?"

"Yes."

Virginia took a calculator from the pocket of
her white lab coat and punched in some figures.
"It's forty-five hundred oyster trays per tank,
times two hundred oysters per tray, times two
tanks. That's almost two million European flat
oysters, which is nearly one and a half million
dollars' worth. We can't afford any mistakes,
and it'll be up to you to see there aren't any."

"I'll do my best." Sylvie could see dozens of
tanks from where she and Virginia stood. What
an operation!

"Your best had better be one hundred percent
if you expect to last long around here."

Sylvie didn't reply. What was there to say to a
remark like that? Debbie had said that Virginia's
insults were just part of her generally unpleasant disposition and weren't aimed at her personally. She vowed to keep that in mind at all times.

As they toured the seafood plantation, Sylvie
discovered that the seaweed she had seen being
harvested was grown from the waste water of
the oyster tanks. The seaweed was then sold to
cosmetic manufacturers, breweries, and food
companies as ingredients for their products.

"Mr. McCloud uses some of it for his lab experiments," Virginia added, waving toward some
dense vegetation on a hill behind the seafood
plantation. Steve's home and research lab must
be there, Sylvie thought, but she certainly
wasn't going to ask Virginia.

By the day's end, Sylvie's mind seemed to
overflow with information. The white plastic

trays where the oysters were raised, the conveyor belts that took them to the big shed to be boxed and flown to the mainland, the electrical systems with the generators and the towering windmills . . . Finally, she gave up trying to remember everything she had observed. She'd met so many workers, both men and women, that their names and faces were just a blur in her memory. But she hadn't met Mahina, the young woman who had answered the telephone Friday morning.

While she and Virginia headed back to the control tower, Sylvie said, "When I called about the job last Friday, a very pleasant woman answered. I believe she said her name is Mahina. Does she work here?"

Virginia frowned. "She's Mr. McCloud's private secretary. Her office is up at the lab." She pointed toward the hill again. "But you probably won't have any occasion to meet her. She never comes down here, and you'll be much too busy to wander off up there." She glanced at her watch. "It's time to call it a day. I know you must be tired."

"Yes, a little," Sylvie admitted. "The first day on a job is always the hardest."

"Your shoes certainly didn't help. Don't wear high heels when you come to work tomorrow, and don't wear a dress either. What with walking over the catwalks and all the equipment you'll be handling, it's best if you wear slacks or jeans."

"Yes, you're right," Sylvie agreed, glancing at the brown smudges on her lime-green dress.

"And that hair! For heaven's sake, cut it or pin it back or braid it. All we'd need is for it to get caught in a conveyor belt." With that, Virginia dismissed her and climbed back up to the tower.

Sylvie stood below and watched Virginia, silhouetted against the plate glass, looking off toward the craggy, tree-covered hill behind the plantation. Then she drove home in the rush-hour traffic that was pouring out from downtown Honolulu.

Though blunt and outspoken, Virginia had been right about the high heels, Sylvie thought, as she settled in the bentwood rocker and rubbed her aching feet. Tomorrow she'd wear jeans and loafers. She could tie her hair back into a ponytail to keep it away from her face—but cut it, never. Let Virginia look elegant and sophisticated with her smart wedge cut. Sylvie's long hair was an integral part of her and she'd keep it that way, with just a gesture toward pulling it back. But she wouldn't braid it, because Steve had said her braid looked silly, that day on the beach. Not that it mattered anymore what he thought. Anyway, she might not see him again for weeks. Virginia had said he often traveled to the mainland, and when he was in Honolulu he spent most of his time at the executive offices of McCloud Enterprises.

But she saw him the next afternoon. She was moving among the plankton tanks to check the pH in two of the tanks, whose alarm lights had gone off in the control tower, when suddenly he stood before her, his head looming above the five-foot walls of the maze of tanks.

"How are you getting along?" he asked. There was a discernible distance in his manner, but his blue-green eyes held hers with an indefinable power.

"I'm learning," she said, "but sometimes I feel it'll be months before I understand everything. So far, I know that if the pH in any tank goes to nine, I have to find out which computer gave the alarm, then make sure the tank's outlets are working properly. I suppose by tomorrow I'll have learned more. Dr. Gamble is teaching me a little at a time."

He nodded and strode away. She stood looking after him, then glanced up toward the tower and found Virginia observing her. When the older woman saw that Sylvie had noticed her scrutiny, she turned away abruptly. For the rest of the afternoon she was more curt than ever, barking orders and losing her patience at the slightest provocation.

However, by the end of the week, Virginia seemed to trust her more and gave her additional duties, so that Sylvie was constantly occupied. Sometimes it seemed she had barely begun working when it was time to leave. She was almost too exhausted every evening to talk with Debbie. It was a satisfying feeling, though; and it gave her a sense of accomplishment and the knowledge of how rewarding it was to be challenged and to succeed.

On Saturday, Sylvie and Debbie took a sight-seeing tour of Pearl Harbor, and visited the Memorial on a Navy shuttle boat. The vast installations at Pearl Harbor were impressive and Sylvie felt a lump in her throat at the thought of December 7, 1941, and of 1,102 sailors entombed that day in their watery grave on the sunken battleship *Arizona*.

On Sunday, Sylvie wrote Fred a long, chatty letter, filled mostly with the details of her job at the seafood plantation.

By Monday, Sylvie found herself looking forward to her job each day. She and Virginia had developed a professional relationship that, if not exactly warm, was pleasant enough.

"I have an appointment at the hairdresser's this afternoon," Virginia told her on Thursday. "Do you think you're ready to take over the whole operation for a while?"

"I think so," Sylvie said with some trepidation.

She was sitting at the computer console, hoping that no red warning lights would flash on, when she heard footsteps climbing the metal stairway to the tower. As the door opened, she looked around and caught her breath, the way she always did when she saw Steve. Today, however, he didn't have that distant manner that he'd had the day she'd seen him down among the plankton tanks.

Seating himself in Virginia's chair behind the metal desk, he cleared his throat and asked very casually, as if he didn't notice that Sylvie was blushing, "Are you busy tonight?"

Astonished, she shook her head. Was he going to ask her for a date? Despite all her determination not to become involved with her employer, she knew that if he asked her, she would go.

"Our prospective clients for the European flats are in Honolulu," he said, his manner neutral and businesslike. Sylvie was torn between relief and disappointment when he continued, "If possible, I'd like you and Dr. Gamble to join me at my private club for dinner, to help entertain these clients. They're a couple from Belgium and the husband's partner. I thought it would make the occasion more festive and relaxed if we were three couples. If you have no objections to giving up your evening to business, that is."

"No, I'd love to," she said, trying to conceal her disappointment.

"I don't mean to press you," he said, being carefully impersonal. "After all, your evenings are your own. If you have other plans, feel free to refuse."

"No, I have no plans." If she'd had other plans, she would have canceled them instantly. This wasn't to be a real date, but at least she would with him, sitting at the same table, hearing his voice. She pulled her ponytail over her shoulder and absently ran her fingers through it.

"Why is you hair pulled back like that?" he demanded.

"It gets in the way when I'm bending over the tanks," she said defensively. What she did with her hair was no concern of his. Suddenly she almost regretted having said she'd go out to dinner with him and his clients. He had an uncanny way of making her feel awkward, defensive, naïve.

"All right, then, if you're sure it won't interfere with your social life, I promise you the meal'll be worth the effort." He stood up to leave, then leaned against Virginia's desk and remarked, "Mr. Copen—that's one of the Belgians—brought a starter of *Thalassiosira,* a type of plankton that appears to fatten up European flats more quickly." He looked down over the plankton tanks. "I see that one of the tanks has been drained and is being refilled. I think it'll be worth trying the *Thalassiosira* to see if we get better results."

He reached for the telephone. "Mahina, tell Ralph to bring down the starter plankton I left on the counter in the lab. It's in a red plastic container. Tell him to add it to tank B7-15 as soon as it's filled."

When he hung up, Sylvie said, "I'd better feed the information into the computer, and perhaps I should contact Dr. Gamble."

With ill-disguised impatience, Steve looked at his watch. "It's almost four o'clock. You run along and do something with that hair. I'll expect you at the Surf Club at eight. I'll feed the information to the computer myself, and Dr. Gamble'll have it at her fingertips first thing in the morning."

"But—"

"Go!" Then as he turned his back to her and sat at the computer console, Sylvie grabbed her purse, shut the door none too gently behind her, and ran downstairs to her car. She'd show him what she could do with "that hair"!

Six

Sylvie spent two hours on her hair. She shampooed it in the shower, letting the warm caress of the water wash away her irritation with Steve, and dried it in the afternoon sunlight while she relaxed on the little upstairs porch.

"Either you're home early or I'm late," Debbie called, running up the wooden steps and kicking off her shoes. "What's up?"

"Some European clients of the plantation are here and Steve's taking them to dinner at the Surf Club. Virginia and I are invited too—as window dressing, I guess." She brushed her hair while she talked, taming the silvery gold strands that danced in the soft breeze.

"The Surf Club!" Debbie whistled under her breath, her hazel eyes wide in her pixie face. "I've never set foot in that exclusive place. What're you going to wear?"

"I thought my white eyelet dress. What do you think?"

Debbie nodded. "Yes, that should strike just the right note for the bright young assistant. You look perfect in it. Are you going to wear your hair down?"

Sylvie twisted her long tresses into a gleaming rope and pulled it forward over her shoulder. "I'd like to put it up," she decided. "Do you remember how Mom used to arrange it for me, coiled on top with a few ringlets hanging loose?"

"I remember. I can help you, but you'll have to curl the ends." Debbie ran a hand through her own cap of short brown curls. "Thou shalt not covet thy roommate's hair, but I'd give a lot if mine could look like that."

Sylvie laughed. "All you have to do is wash it and shake it a little to dry, the way Fred used to do with his when we went swimming." She stared at her friend. "Deb, do you realize that you and Fred look almost like twins? The wavy hair, the dimples, and the hazel eyes—no wonder I like you both so much."

Debbie, who was behind Sylvie, experimenting with her long, shining hair, made no response. Finally she said, "Come on, we'd better go inside and get to work on this if you're going to be ready in time."

They piled Sylvie's shimmering hair on top of her head, then dampened the ends and rolled them on small brush curlers. Next, Sylvie slipped into her white batiste dress. One of her favorites, it was trimmed with wide bands of white eyelet around the scooped neckline, at the hem, and at the wrists below the long, full sleeves. Its simple lines gave an unusual effect of demure sophistication.

While her curls were setting, Sylvie carefully applied a sheer, peachy foundation over her face, lightly dusted pressed transparent powder over it, then gently added a soft rosy blush to her cheekbones.

"You're just gilding the lily, you know," Debbie chided her gently. "You're gorgeous without any of that."

Sylvie laughed. "The lord and master ordered me to 'do something with that hair,' and I'm giving him the whole works. It takes a lot of effort to achieve the natural look."

"You mean the *supernatural* look," Debbie wisecracked. Then she asked, "Are you going to wear any jewelry? Take whatever of mine you want." She gestured grandly. "My treasure is at your command."

"I thought I'd wear my green necklace for a little color."

Debbie held the necklace that Iolani had given Sylvie and studied the irregularly shaped stones. "Good, it's just the right length for that neckline."

"And I'll use green eyeshadow to pick up the green in the necklace," Sylvie said, as she swept color lightly over her eyelids and along the brow line.

"That makes your eyes look enormous! If he could see you now, he'd sweep you away and put a wedding ring on your finger."

"I thought he wasn't the marrying kind."

"What are you talking about? You know Fred's just waiting for you to set the date."

Sylvie met her friend's eyes in the mirror for a moment, then looked away. Fred had been far from her mind and Debbie had read it in her glance.

A touch of brown mascara, clear lip gloss, a few drops of *Je Reviens* at strategic points, and she was ready, quivering inside like a young girl before her first date. Then she firmly reminded herself that this was no date at all, merely a business engagement. Steve had asked her along only because he needed an extra woman to even out the group.

"When is he picking you up?"

"He isn't. I'm supposed to meet everyone there at eight." Sylvie looked at her tiny white-gold watch. It was nearly seven-thirty. "I'd better leave."

"Aren't you going to be fashionably late?"

"You know me better than that. Besides, haven't you heard that punctuality is the quality of kings?" Sylvie slipped on her silver sandals.

"And you look like a princess," Debbie agreed, handing her the matching silver clutch purse. "What a pity to waste all that effort on a bunch of people you don't really care about."

Sylvie picked up her car keys from the coffee table, thinking that she could more than care about one of them, if things were different.

Glowing from Debbie's compliment and from anticipation of the evening ahead, she drove to the Surf Club. Through the sumptuous elegance of the club's dining room, the click of her high heels muffled by the deep pile of the garnet carpeting, Sylvie followed the maître d' to a round table where Steve, handsome in black tie, sat beside Virginia, whose sleek blue silk gown with a deep décolletage made Sylvie's simple white dress look like a young girl's confirmation frock. Casually smoking a cigarette, she observed Sylvie through a veil of smoke with an unspoken message that Sylvie could interpret only as, "You're playing in the big leagues now, and this is my home field."

With a flash of irritation, Sylvie found herself wondering what would happen if she said, "Pardon me, Dr. Gamble, your cleavage is showing." Instead, she smiled at Steve and the European guests. The men stood until she was seated at the table.

When introduced, the Belgian gentlemen bowed, and Mrs. Copen—at least twenty years younger than her husband—elegant in a designer creation of pastel-flowered gray silk, extended her hand. Her ring, a ruby almost as large as her thumbnail and surrounded by diamonds, competed with the shine of the crystal and silver in the candlelight.

While the others had cocktails, Sylvie sipped dry sherry and enjoyed the beautiful view outside the wide windows beside their table. The yacht basin lay just beyond, and the lights on thé yachts reflected like giant fireflies in the still water of the basin. A fifty-foot boat slowly chugged into the basin toward its berth and soon the sound of its engine was covered by the music of a four-piece combo that began playing on the terrace. The music, subdued and inviting, wafted into the dining room and couples began to drift out to dance in the light of the moon and the colorful Japanese lanterns that swayed gently to a rhythm of their own.

Noticing Sylvie's silence, Mrs. Copen flashed her a gracious smile and asked, "Have you ever been to Europe, my dear?"

"No, but I would like to go, someday."

"Not too soon, I hope," quipped Virginia, her tone light but her eyes intense, "at least not till you've earned your vacation."

"Of course not," Sylvie shot back. Boss or no boss, sometimes Virginia was impossible.

"If you do come, perhaps you can visit us," Mrs. Copen suggested. "We live in Lillois, just a few miles from Brussels."

"I'd enjoy that very much, thank you," Sylvie replied, nibbling at her avocado stuffed with crab. She was sipping her white wine very slowly because she was already feeling a bit giddy from the sherry. Château something-or-other, Steve had called it when he ordered. Dry and smooth with a subtle aroma, it dulled the effect of Virginia's cutting remarks.

"I was in Europe last year," Virginia told Madame Copen, her smile excluding Sylvie. "I stayed in France the whole time. I was determined not to wander all over the continent and not remember anything."

Steve remarked that his parents were touring the Aegean Sea on their yacht. "My father has worked so hard for so long, he decided to take some free time and have a real cruise, from Hawaii to Greece through the Panama Canal."

"Speaking of free time . . ." Mr. Van Ness cleared his throat and, fascinated, Sylvie watched his Adam's apple bobbing in his long neck. "Miss Brooke, will you be free tomorrow?"

"No, I'm sorry," she said, not sorry at all. He was trying to be pleasant, but there was a fidgety nervousness about him that she found repugnant.

"I'm sorry, too." He leaned toward her and drummed his fingers on the linen tablecloth. "We have to leave for Japan the following day and I thought perhaps you could show me some of your beautiful Oahu. You must be very proud of this place."

"Miss Brooke is fairly new to the islands," Steve said, "but I'll be glad to show you around if you can wait until afternoon."

"*Merci,* but it would not be the same." Mr. Van Ness bestowed the full splendor of a gallant smile upon Sylvie. His lower teeth were tobacco-stained.

"Of course not," Steve replied easily, "but with me, you'll look at the island's beauty instead of your guide's."

"Perhaps the three of us could rent a car and drive around, starting early in the morning," Mr. Copen suggested, rolling his *r*'s in the distinctive French manner. "What do you think, *chérie*?"

"Of course, that sounds lovely," replied Mrs. Copen.

"I wouldn't hear of that," said Steve. "I'm sorry I have a board meeting tomorrow morning, but my driver will be at your hotel with my car at whatever time you say. He's a native of the islands and will be an excellent guide. If you had more time, I would take you to the other islands over the weekend."

"That's very kind of you. We'll be happy for the use of the car tomorrow, but we're expected in Tokyo the following day," said Mrs. Copen, whose English was more fluent than her husband's.

"As soon as the production of your European flats increases enough, we won't have to buy from Japan anymore," added Mrs. Copen.

"Now, now. No business conversation tonight," said Virginia, smiling sweetly.

They had finished their Maui chicken cooked in coconut milk and served in coconut shells and were awaiting dessert when the band began playing again. Mr. Van Ness asked Sylvie to dance, and she felt she shouldn't refuse. Out on the terrace, he grasped her tightly and steered her among the other couples. In a hoarse voice that was out of rhythm with the music and a little flat, he sang into her ear, *"Non, je ne regrette rien."* He bent his cheek to hers and Sylvie pulled her head back, trying to hide her annoyance and repugnance.

"Do you know the song?" Blissfully unaware of her rejection of him, he beamed down and his pale blue eyes squinted at her.

"No, I'm afraid I've never heard it before."

"It was popular in the forties, I believe, before your time and mine. Yours, at least." He laughed at his own attempted joke. "It was made famous by Edith Piaf—'The Little Sparrow' with the big voice. Do you understand the words?"

"I'm sorry, I never studied French."

" 'No, I regret nothing,' " and on and on, he translated awkwardly, pumping his left arm in time to the music and staring into her eyes until she felt like running off the dance floor. "*Mademoiselle*, I don't regret asking you to take me on a tour of the island, but I do regret you cannot take even one day off from your work."

"I haven't been there long enough to ask for special favors," Sylvie said politely. Even if she had worked at the seafood plantation for ten years, she wouldn't have asked for a day off to spend with Mr. Van Ness. She looked around for a diversion. Virginia was dancing with Mr. Copen, whose bald head reached just to her brow and whose protruding paunch forced him to hold her at a distance, his pudgy hand barely reaching out to her waist. Steve danced with Mrs. Copen. Very slender, and even taller than Virginia, she followed him smoothly. When the music stopped, they all returned to their table for French pastries and coffee.

Steve grinned at Sylvie, as if teasing her about doing her part for the good of the Wai Huihui plantation by dancing with the gawky Belgian. His bantering tone matching the spark of mischief in his eyes as he asked her, "Did you enjoy your . . . dinner?"

"It was memorable," she said, knowing her own eyes mirrored his amused glance. "I especially—"

"It was perfect, darling," Virginia cut in smoothly, "just like everything you do."

The band began to play "The Hawaiian Wedding Song" and, without acknowledging Virginia's remark, Steve rose to his feet. Virginia, her eyes bright and expectant behind heavily mascaraed lashes, started to push back her chair.

But Steve didn't ask her to dance. Neither did he ask Sylvie. Seeming to take for granted that Sylvie would dance with him, he held out his hand to her. With a sense of inevitability, she put her hand in his and he led her toward the terrace, but not before she caught Virginia's angry glance. Then, embarrassed because she had already started to rise, she bent down on the pretext of picking up her napkin from the floor.

Out on the terrace, moving in unison to the haunting music of steel guitar and ukulele, Sylvie and Steve barely spoke. She nestled in his arms and closed her eyes, letting the music wash over her while once again she entered the golden world she had left on Kilauea. He held her gently, his chin lightly touching her temple.

"This is the moment I've waited for," he sang softly with the music, while the pressure of his left hand just above her waist guided her among the other dancers as if the terrace were theirs alone. "Now we are one . . ." the song flowed on. His singing didn't annoy her as Mr. Van Ness's had, but added to the spell of the tropical night. Steve was an excellent dancer. The pattern of his steps was imaginative, yet it was easy to follow because he led with confidence and a grace that was surprising in such a tall, broadshouldered man. He sang in a pleasant baritone. Apparently there was no limit to the number of things he did well. If only the words were his own, and not those of the song, Sylvie wished.

"Ah, there you are," called Mr. Copen, dancing near them with his wife. "Lovely evening isn't it, Miss Brooke?" he asked cheerily. His good humor was infectious, although at that moment Sylvie wished he were ten miles away—or ten thousand. His wife smiled at her with understanding and steered him in another direction.

Reflected lights undulated with the gentle motion of the water of the yacht basin in a liquid dance of their own. Steve pointed them out the her and remarked, "They're like silver cords reaching for the bottom of the sea to catch unwary mermaids. But you're not an unwary mermaid, are you?"

Sylvie interpreted the question as referring to the unattached Belgian. "No, especially when the bait is so unattractive and obvious."

"I'll have to remember that."

"You know very well I'm referring to your client."

"I thought perhaps you meant the song. A little trite and old-fashioned, but effective enough." He grinned down at her and she knew he was teasing her again.

His special blend of smooth sophistication and boyish good humor, the perfect symmetry of his features, his suntan enhanced by his white dinner jacket, the muscular tautness of his body so close to hers . . . she felt that he was about to draw her once more into the magic circle of his charm.

During that miserable flight back from the Big Island, there had been an unspoken understanding between them that they were not going to take each other seriously again. And before that, on that other terrace at the Kona Coast Hotel, with Madame Pele's laughter seeming to mock her in the whisper of the surf, mocking her wish to believe in the power of the green necklace—the same powerless necklace she wore tonight—Steve's clipped words still echoed in her mind, *We'll put today behind us and forget it, as if it hadn't happened.* The gulf between employer and new employee was too great, and for Sylvie, Steve's relationship with Virginia—two manta rays together—lay like a pall over the entire situation. She had decided then that she was going to try to be smarter than one of the little fish.

Now he sparred with her, his warm hand enclosing hers and his ocean-depth eyes searching her face for she knew not what. Was he merely doing his duty as host for the evening's business entertainment? She was trying to think of something impersonal to talk about, then suddenly was lost in the whirlpool of his smile.

The music rescued her by modulating into another number. "They're playing all kinds of old songs tonight," she said. "I've heard that one all my life. My mother used to sing 'Now Is the Hour' sometimes, with a wistful look in her eyes."

"She must have learned it when she was young, during World War Two. The old movies from that period are full of 'good-bye' songs," he said. He glanced toward the musicians with their leis and bright flowered shirts. "Apparently they're doing a Hawaiian set."

"Oh, is this a Hawaiian song?" Here was a safe topic.

"More or less. It's the old Maori farewell song, and the Maoris and original Hawaiians descended from the same stock. Rather fitting, isn't it?" he asked when the music stopped.

He released her and they walked toward their table. *Farewell,* she thought, preceding him as she had when they'd left Kilauea. Farewell to an idealized dream. She had been right. Just now, he had been playing the part of the perfect host, and now he was rejoining his equals and letting his little underling resume her subordinate position.

"Darling, you're just in time," Virginia greeted him, smiling and reaching for his arm with a perfectly manicured hand, as if her camouflaged fury of a short time before never had been. "Our party seems to be breaking up."

"*Monsieur* McCloud, this has been a lovely evening," Mrs. Copen said, "but it is nearly midnight and I do want to tour the island tomorrow."

Sylvie had lost all sense of time while she and Steve had danced on the terrace. "I'll say goodnight too," she said, picking up her silver purse and standing up to leave. "My boss wouldn't accept any excuses if I were late tomorrow." Virginia rewarded her with an angry glare.

"Let me accompany you to your car." Mr. Van Ness already was at her side.

"I'll have the cars brought around," Steve said firmly, signaling their waiter.

Mrs. Copen excused herself, and Virginia, with steel in her voice, commanded, "Come along, Sylvie," and swept after Mrs. Copen toward the ladies' room.

Sylvie felt that she had no choice but to follow.

In the lavishly appointed lounge, all silver, blue velvet, and mirrors, Virginia busied herself powdering her face and touching up her scarlet lipstick until Mrs. Copen had left. Then she turned to Sylvie with such naked fury in her eyes that Sylvie retreated and leaned against the carved arm of a settee.

"You idiot!" Virginia spat. "What do you think you're doing?"

"I beg your pardon?"

" 'I beg your pardon,' " mimicked Virginia.

"You know very well what I'm talking about, and I'm warning you right now. Lay off!"

"I really don't know what you mean." Sylvie's restrained response and neutral mask concealed her wariness and her growing fear of Virginia's malice. "If you mean the decision about the new—"

"Come off it! You couldn't be that stupid, not even if you tried. I mean Steve McCloud, of course. *Mr.* McCloud to you, dear."

Sylvie was too stunned to reply. She searched her mind. Had she called Steve by his first name? No, she had carefully avoided addressing him by any name since their return from the Big Island. After their conversation on the terrace of the Kona Coast Hotel, she wasn't comfortable calling him by his first name, but addressing him as *Mr.*, after their kisses on Kilauea, seemed stiff and dishonest.

"Keep your sugary 'poor little me' smiles for the men in your own class. You're way out of his! Don't let me catch you flirting with him again."

Sylvie felt herself reddening and turned away, attempting to regain her composure while she pretended to inspect her hair in the mirror. Virginia's glare confronted her in an infinity of images that skipped from one mirrored wall to another. She faced her accuser again and said softly, "Dr. Gamble, you have no right. My private life is my own. I'm not sure what you're talking about, but I'm trying to understand. I drove myself here in my own car and I'm going home alone. I was invited only to round out the party, and I thought it was my duty to accept, since it had to do with the plantation."

"Was it your duty to entice him to dance the wedding song with you?"

"You know I didn't," she said firmly.

"I saw you do it!" Virginia's eyes were slits in her angry face. Never before in Sylvie's life had she been the object of such animosity.

"The song was just a coincidence," Sylvie protested. "I danced with him just as I did with Mr. Van Ness and you did with Mr. Copen."

"A fine coincidence that was. I'm not blind. You signaled to him. How very romantic! Don't you realize by now that I'm going to marry him? You keep your hands off him—if you want to keep your job, that is."

Sylvie couldn't believe this was happening. How could the woman who now confronted her, her ivory skin livid with anger in contrast to her sculpted black hair and the scarlet slash of her lips, be so beautiful on the outside and so twisted and ugly inside?

She decided to try again. "I haven't flirted with him, Dr. Gamble. You must know that. I'm sorry if you're disappointed because he danced that particular song with me. If it had a special meaning for you that it doesn't have for me, I—"

"Why, you little—"

"Please, Dr. Gamble, let me finish." Sylvie had to get through to Virginia. She didn't want to jeopardize her job because of the other woman's mistaken jealousy. She breathed deeply and tried to control her shaky voice. "It would be against my principles to have any sort of relationship with a man I work for. It's also against my principles to flirt with any man who is married or engaged." She couldn't help glancing at Virginia's left hand. There was no diamond there.

Virginia saw the look and the quickly averted eyes. Without another word, she stalked out.

Sylvie sat on the velvet settee and trembled

amid the harsh echoes of the scene Virginia had thrust upon her.

Perhaps what Virginia had said was true. She liked and needed her job, and there was no point in flirting with a man who was beyond her reach. Sylvie wasn't one of the new breed of young women who aggressively went after the men they wanted. If Steve had wanted her, the moves would have been up to him. And his moves on the volcano had only warned her to retreat. And even that was all past. He was involved with Virginia, and that was that. Perhaps aggressive women appealed to him. If that was the case, it would definitely eliminate Sylvie.

But . . . what about their seemingly timeless dance together on the terrace tonight? While she applied fresh lip gloss, Sylvie found herself wondering what would happen if she could find an opening at one of the local hospitals, so she'd not be working for Steve's company. If she weren't his employee, would he feel free to seek her out and let her know how he felt?

Again, there was Virginia. How could she keep forgetting, even for a moment, especially right after Virginia had so forcefully staked out her territory? And what about Fred? She dismissed Fred from her mind as one dismisses a gnat trying to alight on a peach, then chided herself for disposing of him so casually. She had to stop worrying about things she couldn't control, such as Steve's feelings, or Fred's, or her own, for that matter. She would sort out her own feelings later, when she could think more clearly.

Her party was waiting for her by the dining-room entrance. They all strolled outside. While the others stood chatting in a little group, Steve walked with her to her little yellow Toyota, which was dwarfed by his white Jaguar parked behind it.

A frown between his eyebrows was softened by the concern in his eyes. "Are you all right, Sylvie?"

"Yes," she murmured, aware of Virginia's presence only a few feet away. She avoided looking at him and said lightly, "The wine and the heat . . ." She left the sentence unfinished. What heat? The night was perfect.

"Yes, the heat." He opened the door.

"Thank you," she said. "It's been an evening to remember."

"And for me." She was too spent to try to read any special meaning into his brief rejoinders.

Driving away, she could see him standing in front of the Surf Club beside Virginia's red Porsche.

She sighed. The evening that had begun so pleasantly had ended in disaster. And tomorrow morning, at work, she would have to face Virginia.

Seven

Sylvie spent a restless, uneasy night. Twice she got up and looked toward Virginia's condominium, but the place was dark, the lanai was empty, and there was no white Jaguar parked outside. Sylvie realized that she should know Virginia well enough by now to ignore her nasty sarcasm, but she could not dismiss or justify tonight's scene in the lounge. As for Steve, his face had no business floating in and out of her fragmented dreams, mocking her denials to Virginia. It was Fred who should be in her dreams—Fred, who loved her.

"Wake up, sleepyhead, it's seven o'clock!" Debbie was shaking her shoulder.

Sylvie sat bolt upright. The morning sun gilded the room and a bird hooted outside with a junglelike sound.

"Have I overslept? I mustn't be late for work, today of all days. She'd kill me." Sylvie darted to the closet and snatched up a pair of white slacks and a white knit top. She brushed her hair and tied it back with a soft green scarf that matched her necklace. Not too practical an outfit for the lab, perhaps, but the white was spectacular with her honey-gold tan, and today she needed every morale booster she could muster.

"Slow down," Debbie cautioned. "You have plenty of time. But what's the deal? You're usually the first one up. Didn't I hear you come in before one?"

Not waiting for an answer, Debbie dressed quickly and took fresh mangoes from the refrigerator for their breakfast.

Sylvie flopped down at the dinette table. "I just didn't sleep well. I don't know why I was so restless."

"I should've let you talk when you came in. That would have unwound you. But I didn't say anything then because I knew I'd want to wake clear up and hear all about the Surf Club if we started talking. How was it?"

"Out of this world. Everything was terrific until . . ."

"Until?"

"That Virginia. She's an absolute witch, and I have this strange feeling in the pit of my stomach. I wish I didn't have to see her today at all."

"Did she drink too much and fly her true colors even with Steve there?"

"No, she was charming when he was within earshot. But you should have heard her in the ladies' lounge."

"Come on, Syl, don't make me pull the words out of your mouth one by one! What happened?"

"Oh, nothing much." Sylvie's voice took on an unaccustomed sarcasm. "She *only* ordered me to stay away from Steve because he belongs to her and she's going to marry him."

"That's nothing new." Debbie laughed.

"She's been after him since before I knew her, and as far as I can tell, he hasn't asked her yet."

"It's not funny," Sylvie insisted. "Remember, I have to work with her. She threatened to fire me."

"Why are you making her jealous, then?"

Sylvie slammed her teaspoon down on the table. "I'm not! That's what's driving me up the wall. I'm not doing a thing. I don't flirt with him. I don't lead him on. I'm just as proper as I know how to be."

"I'm sorry, Syl. In a way, it's really sad. You're so beautiful and young, and Virginia's no spring chicken. She's had a hard life. Her family was poor—and I mean dirt poor. But Virginia was smart, and she worked hard. She got a college scholarship, but she had to wait tables all through school to make it. By that time, her mother had cancer, and Virginia had to help."

"That's hard to believe, when I think of the way she lives now. The Porsche, the accessories—and you should have seen the dress she was wearing last night! It would cost half a month's salary for you or me."

"That's all part of the image she's trying to project," Debbie explained. "Her top-drawer job, her lavish lifestyle—those things don't make her feel secure. She's like a tigress who's clawed her way almost to the top, and the only thing that'll satisfy her now is to marry some good-looking, wealthy man who has the social position she can't achieve on her own. There aren't too many like Steve floating around unattached, and Virginia knows she isn't getting any younger."

Sylvie sat motionless during Debbie's recital. "I still don't see why she can't act like a human being. She has a good career and all the material possessions anyone could want."

"I already told you what it is she wants!"

While they cleared the table, Debbie said, "Can't you understand? Steve's the only thing that's important to her now—the only thing she wants but can't seem to get. But believe me, she'll do anything to keep you out of her way where Steve's concerned."

Sylvie nodded. She understood, but she felt no sympathy. "I really must go now, Deb," she said. "Thanks for filling me in. I'll see you tonight."

As Sylvie waited at a traffic signal, she glanced at her watch and realized she needed to hurry or she'd be late. After the scene last night, Virginia would not take her tardiness lightly. When the light turned green, she stepped on the accelerator. Except for a futile grinding sound, nothing happened. Then she looked at the gas gauge. It registered empty. Since this was her first car, she wasn't accustomed to watching for things like that as closely as she should. Now she didn't know what to do. Though it seemed ridiculous, all she could think of was to stand beside the car and look helpless in the hope that someone might stop.

She had barely finished raising the hood as a distress signal when the roar of a motorcycle descended upon her.

"Hi, missy! *Heaha ka pilikia?*" It was her old friend Sam. Bare-chested as usual, with his bright shirt unbuttoned, to Sylvie at the moment he looked like Sir Galahad. Seeing her uncomprehending expression, he repeated, "*Heaha ka pilikia*—what's the trouble?"

After she'd told him, he left with a roar and was back in a few minutes. From the back of his motorcycle he produced a gas can, which he emptied into her tank.

"*Aole pilikia,* missy—no trouble! Next time,

you watch the gas!" He waved away her thanks and offer of payment and was gone as suddenly as he had come.

Sylvie drove faster than usual and arrived at the control tower just ten minutes behind schedule. Knowing that Virginia would be furious, Sylvie stood in the doorway for a moment and looked in. Virginia stood staring down at the plankton farm.

When Sylvie closed the door softly behind her, Virginia yelled without turning around, "You're late!"

"I'm sorry. It's just a few minutes, but I'll make it up during my lunch hour." That woman! Sylvie had made a point of arriving at least five minutes early every day, and now, the one morning she missed, Virginia was enraged. But after last night, what else could she expect?

Virginia wheeled around to face her. Contempt filled every word when she said, "All in white again, and wearing those cheap green beads."

Sylvie's hand flew to her throat. "I . . ."

"Never mind," Virginia shouted. "The point is—what did you put in that tank?" She pointed toward B7-15 as if its contents were poison.

Sylvie tried to control her anger by counting slowly to ten before replying, but by the time she had reached three, Virginia had dashed across the room and shoved her against the closed door.

"You have no right to make that type of decision without consulting me first!" Virginia's face was red, and a vein stood out on her forehead as she fumed, "You little bitch! Get out of here and don't let me see your simpering face again!"

As Virginia whirled around to return to her desk, she tripped on the stool by the computer control panel. A piercing siren screamed from the top of the tower. In the instant of falling against the controls and groping to regain her balance, Virginia had hit an alarm button.

Sylvie, who had been astonished by Virginia's precipitous attack, finally realized what was upsetting her boss. She cried over the screech of the siren, "All the information is in the computer! Steve punched it in last night!"

"That's not the point of the matter. You knew where I was. You should have called me."

"I planned to tell you in the lounge last night, but you . . . you know how you behaved."

Virginia's livid face was again scant inches from Sylvie's and Sylvie wanted to back away, to explain that it had been Steve's decision, not hers. But a closed door was at her back, and for a brief instant she feared that Virginia would slap her face.

Sylvie had taken enough abuse. No job, no matter how important to her, was worth this kind of insult and humiliation. To work any longer for this irrational, jealous woman, who would give her neither the benefit of the doubt nor the chance to explain, would be impossible. Suffocated by a torrent of accusations storming around her head, Sylvie turned around and opened the door behind her. She rushed from the control tower, pursued by Virginia's stream of invectives, shouted in a harsh voice over the wail of the siren and echoing down the stairs and into the parking lot, where Sylvie fumbled to unlock her Toyota.

". . . And don't you dare ask for a reference, you incompetent fool. You'll never get one from me. I've never had such an inept and disloyal . . ."

Sylvie slammed the car door and drove off. She paid no attention to the crowd of plantation workers summoned by the alarm, who stood nearby, looking from the departing car to the top of the tower in silent amazement.

Still in a turmoil when she got home, Sylvie took a bundle of mail from the box and, upstairs, dropped it on the coffee table beside the morning paper. She was in no mood for a stack of junk mail right now. She couldn't rest or even call to tell Debbie what had happened. She herself was only barely beginning to realize its significance. Sylvie Brooke had been fired from her first job, and through no fault of her own.

She paced the apartment, from kitchen to bedroom to living room, wondering what she should do now. To search for a new job would be difficult. Although she was innocent of any duplicity, the only local reference she had was a bad one. Her only solution would be to omit the seafood plantation job from future employment applications. That would be simpler than trying to explain.

She picked up the morning paper from the coffee table but couldn't stop her pacing long enough to check the want-ads. Hardly realizing what she was doing as she tried to calm herself, she plunged into a flurry of sweeping floors, washing windows, and scrubbing cabinets. She changed the beds and, surprised by her own strength, even turned the mattresses.

After four hours, the apartment was spotless. Even the linen closet had been straightened, with all the towels and sheets refolded in neat piles. Sylvie fixed herself a cup of coffee and collapsed into the rocking chair, her head back and her eyes closed. The physical exertion had relaxed her, and she rocked slowly, reassuring herself that she could stretch her two-week paycheck until she found something else. If she could just find another job soon, she'd be all right.

If she didn't get another job, her mother would send her the money for a ticket home, and she would be welcomed with love and attention. The prodigal daughter would return to Oklahoma City, having proved that she couldn't make it on her own. There would be no recriminations—but sometimes, just by being nice, people could drive home a lesson more effectively than if they said, "I told you so." She would have to handle that as best she could, if it happened.

Fred would certainly be happy to have her back. But would it be fair to him to offer herself now—discouraged, defeated, and ready to marry him just because she had failed to do what she had set out to accomplish on her own?

She picked up the mail from the coffee table where she had tossed it when she first came in and riffled the pile. There was a letter from Fred. How comfortingly familiar that sprawling script looked to her right now. It was as if her need had summoned him to her side. She tore open the envelope and read:

Dear Sylvie,

I know I promised not to press you any more to come home. But I love you and need you, and I miss you more than I can say. I've even been considering flying out there to see you. Just to hold you again would help me endure our separation. If you want me to come, just call me and I'll catch the first available flight.

Please say hello to Debbie for me—but hopefully I'll see you soon and can tell her myself.

> *All my love,*
> *Fred*

With the letter open in her lap, Sylvie leaned back and closed her eyes. Dear Fred, so loving and uncomplicated. Just reading his letter made her feel secure and cared for.

She discovered she was brushing tears from her eyes with the tip of the green scarf that still held her hair, and stroking the smooth stones of Iolani's necklace. How chaotic life would be if she married an independent, authoritative man like the president of McCloud Enterprises! And how had her thoughts of Fred's love become filled with blue-green eyes, a mocking smile in a sun-bronzed face, and memories of a few kisses on Kilauea and one dreamy dance on the Surf Club terrace?

Suddenly the telephone rang, drawing her back to the present. She picked up the receiver and Fred's letter fluttered to the floor, unnoticed. "Hello?"

"Sylvie?"

"Yes, Mr. McCloud." She would know his voice anywhere.

"Steve, please. I heard about what happened and I can't begin to apologize."

"Thank you, but that isn't necessary."

"Yes, it is. You were right yesterday. I should have told Virginia about my decision. Or let you do it, as you wanted. I didn't realize how she would react. You must know her better than I do."

He didn't understand that Virginia's resentment included what had happened last night at the Surf Club, as well as the situation at the seafood plantation.

"These things blow over. . . . Sylvie?"

She didn't answer. What was there to say? Virginia, with all her faults, was nevertheless a brilliant scientist and an essential part of McCloud Enterprises. Sylvie, on the other hand, had barely begun to be of any real use at the seafood plantation. Two weeks was not long enough for anyone to become indispensable in a new position. She knew it and Steve knew it.

"Are you still there?" His voice was concerned and kind.

"Yes," she whispered.

"I don't want you to worry about your job. Promise me."

"I'm not worrying about a job I don't have anymore. She fired me, didn't she tell you?"

Surely he wasn't going to ask her to go back to Wai Huihui and work with Virginia again. She'd rather go home to Oklahoma City in defeat than stay here and try to get along with that unreasonable, selfish, insulting woman. Even the exhausting physical work of cleaning the apartment had not dissipated her anger at Virginia. If Steve did marry her, he would regret it for the rest of his life.

"She did, and that's why I want to talk to you. Are you free tonight?"

"There's really nothing to talk about. I'm not blaming you, Mr. McCloud." He wasn't going to persuade her to return to Wai Huihui—not even if it was the last job on earth.

"Sylvie . . . it's *Steve*, remember. Please."

"I'm not blaming you, Steve," she said docilely. "But surely you don't think I would be interested in being Dr. Gamble's assistant ever again. If I don't find something else soon, I'll go—"

"That's why we must talk," he interrupted. She was right in thinking he considered her only a sweet young thing, a nonentity who'd have nothing of importance to say. But he was trying to be kind. She would listen. "I'm not suggesting you go back there. I've already apologized for not following your suggestion yesterday. Now I want to apologize for Dr. Gamble's behavior.''

"I didn't blame you for the way she acted."

"She's my employee, Sylvie, so I'm responsible for what she does. Please, let's forget about her right now. I know you're upset, and you have a right to be. Just put what happened this morning out of your mind.''

Yes, Sylvie told him silently, *and last night in the lounge at the Surf Club, too. You don't know about that.*

"Don't worry about finding a job," he continued. "Not right now. I'll pick you up at seven-thirty and we'll have dinner together. I want to discuss something with you in a relaxed atmosphere. All right?''

She had nothing to lose. He had many contacts in Honolulu and probably meant to help her. If he did, that would square things with his own conscience for contributing to her dismissal. And now that she wasn't his employee any longer, the idea of dinner alone with him tonight was appealing—even if the specter of Virginia would accompany them. Why shouldn't she make the most of his invitation and have a pleasant evening? He was urbane, handsome, and interesting. She remembered what Debbie had said—he could have any woman he wanted. *But not me,* she thought, *not me.*

"All right," she said, "I'll be ready at seven-thirty. Where are we going?''

"That's a surprise, but I guarantee you won't be disappointed.''

So far, his choices never had disappointed her. She had asked where they were going only to have an idea of what to wear. If the Surf Club was any indication, she'd better be prepared. Her beige silk suit with the paisley blouse would look appropriate anywhere. It was dressy but not too dressy. With her gold butterfly pin on her shoulder, it would take her to the most exclusive restaurant or to a job interview.

When Debbie came home, Sylvie was dressed and almost ready. Debbie put down the packages she carried and surveyed Sylvie, who sat before the mirror arranging her hair in a chignon at the nape of her neck, with soft curls framing the cameo of her face.

"Are you going out? As if I had to ask."

Sylvie turned from the mirror. "Debbie, I lost my job."

"Sure, so you're going out to celebrate becoming penniless. Right?" Debbie plopped down on her bed. "What's going on?"

"I'm serious. She fired me, and now Steve's taking me out to dinner to talk about it. He seems to think he can help."

Sylvie's voice trembled when she began telling her roommate about her morning, but by the time she had finished, with Debbie howling like the siren atop the control tower and interjecting satirical comments about Virginia, they were both laughing.

"So there she was, the queen of the plantation, left alone with plankton all over her face." Debbie grinned. "It's just such a hilarious picture, that siren wailing and Virginia screeching at you from the top of the tower, giving the employees a ringside seat while she made a fool of herself. . . ."

"Debbie Leighter, you ought to be on TV. You could cheer anybody up, no matter how miserable they were." By now Sylvie found herself actually looking forward to going out with Steve.

As he drove Sylvie through the rosy early evening, Steve didn't refer to the morning events. Soon they sat facing each other at a table in La

Ronde, atop the Ala Maona Building, while the restaurant revolved ever so slowly, spreading Honolulu like a cyclorama four hundred feet below. He drank scotch and water and she sipped sherry as they scanned the sweep of the sea's horizon and watched the gradual procession of landmarks while the lights of the city blinked on, one after another, in the deepening dusk. Gradually, peace enfolded her.

Bemused, she barely noticed the progression of the excellent dinner he had ordered for her, through tossed green salad, tender crown rib with baked potato, and pineapple sherbet. Over coffee, he cleared his throat. *Here it comes,* she thought.

"You remember my telling you about the various enterprises of my company that day?"

That day on the island of Hawaii, the day her dreams were born and died with the red-hot splendor of a burst of molten lava. She remembered every moment of that day. She nodded and continued sipping her coffee. She didn't look at him.

"The research laboratory is really my avocation. I told you my technician was leaving. Her doctor has ordered her off her feet immediately, so she won't be back Monday. I haven't talked to Mrs. Dutton about a replacement. Somehow, I hoped . . ."

He sat there looking at the harbor while the Japanese waitress refilled their coffee cups and cleared away their dishes.

Then he continued, "You know, I wanted you to work for me from the beginning. But there was no way for me to offer you a job after I learned that Virginia had found you and wanted you for her assistant."

It was Sylvie's turn to look out over the water where the lights on countless boats were like stars in the deep-blue chiffon of the sea. She searched her mind for a reply. She didn't want to sound flippant, and it would be so easy to make a caustic remark about Virginia. Finally she said softly, "She doesn't want me anymore, and, as I told you, the situation with her has become impossible."

"Yes, of course. But I'm talking about your working for me in my research lab. The salary is better than at Wai Huihui."

Sylvie waved her hand as if at this point the salary were immaterial.

"Let me finish, Sylvie." The blue-green depths of his eyes, serious and intent under the classic arch of his eyebrows, held hers. "The most important requirement for this particular job—naturally besides your technical skills, which I understand are excellent—is absolute discretion."

"Of course. As you surely know, with my hospital training, that was stressed from the very beginning. The patients' right to privacy . . . why, medical technicians could be sued for divulging privileged information."

"Yes, but that's not exactly what I'm talking about. You see, sometimes I work on a project for months, until it's perfected, then I patent it. If my competitors were to find out what I was working on, they could rush through with their own research, perhaps using my methods and my trials and errors to their own advantage, and patent the product before I could. Months of effort would be wasted."

"Yes, I see the importance of discretion." Sylvie knew the painstaking tests involved in research and what a disappointment it would be to have so much labor go to waste, even without the added consideration of financial loss.

"I'm not doubting your trustworthiness," he

assured her. "If I did, I wouldn't be talking to you about my work right now. But I do want to explain further, if I'm not boring you."

"Of course you aren't." As if anything he might say could bore her!

"We needn't talk about my current project tonight. Monday'll be time enough, assuming you accept the position. What I want to explain is this. My father is chairman of the board of McCloud Enterprises. He's rather reactionary, and it's been a struggle for me to persuade him to diversify. I set up the research lab with my own personal capital, and I use my earnings from that as I wish. It's my own thing. If the lab loses money, I don't have to answer to anyone about it. I think I've told you, that was how I built the seafood plantation, and it's proven quite profitable. The manufacturing part of the laboratory, on the outskirts of the city, was built with the profits from the seafood plantation."

Sylvie was fascinated. It was a chain of successes. This only confirmed her impression that Steve was not merely the son of a wealthy plantation owner, content to luxuriate in the shadow of his father's accomplishments and drift along with a token position in the family business. "How many products have you patented?" Her brown eyes, outlined by curving dark lashes, were wide with interest.

"Seven, in the past four years. And we have clients all over the mainland with standing orders for the manufacturing lab. Our patents safeguard the products. But one time last year, a culture medium that was nearly ready for patenting was registered instead by Diamond Head Scientific Labs."

"That must have been discouraging. Was it a coincidence?"

"Probably. You hear of this type of thing hap-

pening every so often in the scientific world. I
don't see how the formula could have been stolen. Rosina has been my technician for five
years, and I'm sure she's trustworthy. Mahina,
my secretary, I've known since she was born.
She's Iolani's granddaughter. And I don't discuss my research with anyone else."

"I see why you stressed confidentiality, and I
appreciate your faith in me. If you're offering me
the chance to be Rosina's replacement, you can
trust me not to say anything about your research to anyone. I'll be proud to work with
you." The position sounded perfect. Research
was her favorite field. As for the personal angle,
this evening was going well enough, and with all
of Steve's varied business interests, he wouldn't
be spending much time in the lab. When he was
there, she assured herself, she could handle it.
She just wouldn't let herself think of him in a
personal way. Realizing that she was leaning toward him in her eagerness, she straightened
quickly and stared at her coffee cup as if it were
the first one she had ever seen.

"Good. That's settled, then." His casual smile
giving no indication that he had noticed her embarrassment, he leaned back in his black leather
chair. "Would you like a liqueur?"

"Yes, thank you. Chartreuse would be fine."

As she sipped the aromatic green liqueur and
he drank his cognac, he said, "Let's call this a
celebration. You'll be doing the kind of work you
want, and I have a new technician, starting right
now."

"Right now?"

Steve laughed. "You're still on the payroll of
McCloud Enterprises, aren't you? I meant to get
across the idea that you won't lose any salary
from the tiff with Virginia this morning." It had
been much more than a tiff, but she didn't cor-

rect him. "Just come to work Monday morning at eight o'clock at the lab. I'll show you around before I leave. Usually I'm not there much, but the lab has a direct line to my private telephone at company headquarters downtown, and Mahina can always reach me with the beeper." He showed her a tiny square box that had been attached to his belt, then clipped it back in place.

"That's like the ones the doctors at the hospital wore, when I was taking my training."

He nodded agreement, then asked, "Are there any questions?"

There it was, that briskness that had entered his voice after she'd told him about her job that evening at the Kona Coast Hotel. Now she thought how good it was to spend time with him tonight, just as a man and a woman who enjoyed each other's company. "I've never been to the lab," she said, managing to achieve an impersonal manner like his, "but it's been pointed out to me from the seafood plantation. It's up on the hill behind the grove of palms and the heavy jungle growth, isn't it?"

"Yes. You come in the same way as if you were going to the plantation, but follow the road as far as it'll take you. You can't miss it." He looked at his watch.

Here she was again, his employee. No dancing, no light conversation, and certainly no romance. It was nearly midnight and time to leave. Nothing was destined to develop between her and this special, handsome man whose magnetism reached out and enfolded her like the warmth of a glowing fire. Her relief at still having a job was tempered by that thought. It was just not meant to be. McCloud Enterprises stood between them, as it had when she was working at Wai Huihui. Also, Virginia had a prior claim on Steve.

Eight

Perched on a low hill overlooking the far blue reaches where the Pacific Ocean met the sky, Steve McCloud's sprawling, Polynesian-style house was almost hidden by trees and flowering shrubs. Sylvie parked in the circular driveway early Monday morning and approached the veranda, which wrapped around the house like a sun-warmed embrace.

Steve, handsome in a pearl-gray business suit, the color of his tie identical to that of his eyes, met her on this veranda where comfortable-looking rattan and bamboo furniture gave an atmosphere of old Hawaii. The chairs and settees were cushioned with bright, sunny prints, and the ocean just below the house shimmered with every color of the blue-green spectrum, from aqua to deep turquoise to sapphire.

"I see you had no trouble finding my retreat." His eyes, welcoming her, had drawn their color from the sea and infused it with the heat of the sun.

"No, I knew the way." She smiled at him. "The view here is beautiful."

"Yes, that's why I chose this site. Come in, we'll walk through the house to get to the lab at the back. But you see, the way this is built, you'll have the same view from there." He led her through a series of spacious rooms.

Sylvie had a sensation of floating above the ocean, which, visible through undraped floor-to-ceiling windows in each room, dominated the house. The interior walls and the low dividers between rooms, which made the place seem to borrow light and vistas from within itself, were painted a soft, luminous, pearly blend of palest gray and ivory. There were fresh flowers everywhere in shades of coral and pink, and coral throw cushions on the sectional sofas, which were upholstered in suede so soft a shade of plum as to seem neutral, gave the living room a rosy ambiance.

He preceded her, and Sylvie was admiring his walk, athletic yet graceful, like that of a fencer or a gymnast, when a collection of prisms hanging in the wall of windows in the living room attracted her attention. The prisms sent rainbows dancing on the ceiling. The handsome sophistication of the decor was deceptively simple. A small fortune in crystal bowls and polished silver tankards adorned the floor-to-ceiling inset shelves in the dining room. Sylvie lagged behind, admiring the surroundings.

"Are you coming?" Steve waited for her in the family room beside a huge, black leather sofa that faced an oversized wall television screen.

"Everything here is so beautiful," Sylvie said, admiring the contrast between the luxurious modern decor and the more rustic outside architecture with its peaked Polynesian roof.

"You can reach the lab either this way,

through the house, or by driving to the back and going there directly," he said. "The living and working quarters are connected and you can use either door. Just remember, if you leave after Mahina, lock the connecting doors. The lab must be locked without fail when none of the three of us is here."

"I won't forget," she promised, taking the key he handed her. They proceeded through an office with a modern black and chrome desk, red typewriter and telephone, and black and chrome filing cabinets lining the walls. Hanging plants gave it an outdoor feeling, and it could be entered from the encircling veranda. No one was in the office.

"Mahina comes in at eight-thirty," Steve said. "I wanted you here early today so I could have more time to show you around before going downtown to headquarters."

"I'll try to remember everything so you'll have to tell me only once," she said, and was rewarded by a sudden smile.

"You sound like a little girl on the first day of school," he said, chuckling, and hope fluttered within her. Perhaps he had decided to let friendship bud between them instead of considering her just as an employee. The spark of warmth was extinguished at once when he launched into a detailed description of his current project. Would she never learn, never stop dreaming?

Steve explained that the project was a new antimicrobial removal medium. "You've probably used antimicrobial removal devices— A.R.D.s—before, in the labs at school."

"Yes, of course," she said, thinking of the counters scarred from hard use by so many students, acid-stained floors, and all the bustle and confusion. What a difference there was here, with soft blue countertops and a deeper blue floor. The walls and cabinets were eggshell white. All the instruments and glassware gleamed. And the view from the sliding glass door was breathtaking.

Steve showed her the location of everything she would need, but it was almost impossible to concentrate when he was so close to her. She found herself struggling to wrest her attention away from his warmth and his masculinity.

"Usually, resins are used to remove antibiotics that might inhibit the growth of microbes in a blood culture specimen," he continued, clearly unaware of the effect he had on her.

"I know," she responded, wanting to show him how well she knew the theories behind all laboratory procedures. After all, studying for her registry and getting her official degree as a medical technologist was still quite fresh in her mind. "If a patient has been on antibiotic therapy before his disease has been diagnosed, the bacteria can't be cultured and the doctor can't know what kind of disease the patient has." *There, that should do it!* she thought.

"Precisely." He picked up a small, unlabelled vial with an aluminum cap, which looked exactly like the vials Sylvie had used during her training, and held it out to her. She took it, her fingers trembling when his hand brushed hers. Apparently he didn't notice. He was smiling at her as he said, "I've used a new kind of resin—from the ohia tree, do you remember?"

"Yes," she said, feeling her face grow warm as she recalled the legend of the two lovers. "When the red lehuas are picked, it rains because they cannot bear to be separated," he had told her.

She turned abruptly and looked at a cove where the waves broke gently on a little sliver of beach a hundred feet below. That cove was only a few hundred yards from the tiny cove where

Steve had stood, waving his arms and shouting in a vain attempt to warn her. It seemed so long ago, the day when he had rescued her, his strong hand forcing the breath back into her body just as his strong arms had made her come alive at Kilauea.

She forced herself to ask lightly, "And what happens when sap is taken from the ohia tree for the resin?"

Steve laughed outright. "I wonder. Perhaps he's too weak to hold his princess and lets her drop over the rim of Kilauea's crater into the fire pit!"

Sylvie felt she was on shaky ground. This was no time for talk of lovers and old legends. If she was to keep this new job, she must steer him back to discussion of his project. "You were telling me about the resin," she said.

He glanced at her and cleared his throat, then continued, as if he hadn't digressed, "We use resin and powdered seaweed to speed up the binding process. Now we have to keep experimenting with the blood cultures." He opened an incubator to reveal a row of numbered vials, then showed her the neatly written records Rosina had left behind. "All indications are that it'll be much more efficient than what is currently available."

Sylvie leaned on the counter, trying to absorb all the information. As he was pointing out an entry in a logbook, his hand touched her hair lightly, as if it were a fine silken cloth he wanted to appraise. She drew back quickly, and he turned his back to her and stood at the sliding glass door, watching a distant ship cruising toward Honolulu.

The clack of a typewriter in the adjoining office intruded on the silence in the lab. Steve's voice was carefully controlled as he said, "Mahina's here now. As I told you before, she always knows where I can be reached, and she'll help you when I'm not here." He gave her a level look and continued, "As for the current project, Rosina and I have already perfected the combination of seaweed and resin. The producton lab is ready to gear up for manufacture when I give them the go-ahead."

He thumbed through a looseleaf notebook, then handed it to her. "This is the formula, on page seventeen. It's hidden, disguised among other notations so that no unauthorized person would know where to look for it. All we need now are about two weeks of trials."

"And then what'll happen?" The thought of helping test a discovery was even more exciting than Sylvie had imagined when she'd dreamed of working in research.

"If our experiments are successful, we're in business. The only thing left to do will be to apply for the patent. We'll send the data to Washington, D.C., and the patent attorney will take care of registering it for us."

"Where do I get the blood for the cultures?" Sylvie was beginning to share his enthusiasm for the project and was eager to begin her part in it.

"It'll be delivered twice a week. Mahina knows about it." He pointed to the first page of the looseleaf notebook, where all the steps of the method were outlined. "All you have to do is follow these instructions and enter the results in the logbook. Any questions?"

Sylvie scanned the instructions. They were identical to the procedures she had used at the lab at school, except that the time for each step had been shortened. When Steve showed her the cabinet where the vials were stored, her shoulder brushed against his arm as she stood on tiptoe to look.

Not looking at her, he said, "I have to go now. I'll probably see you very seldom. Come, I want you to meet Mahina." He strode through the open door, introduced the two young women, and left with firm, quick steps.

Mahina was about Sylvie's age, but there the similarity ended. The secretary was tall and statuesque, while Sylvie was petite. With her full lips, dark eyes, and wavy black hair, Mahina seemed a picture of the original Hawaiians who had come to the islands from Polynesia centuries ago. Her teeth shone brightly in her dusky, friendly face.

"At last, Mahina," Sylvie greeted her. "I've wanted to meet you ever since we spoke on the phone that day, just before I started work at the seafood plantation."

Mahina's laughter rang clear like a silver bell in a mountain meadow. "I have too. I really wanted to warn you about Dr. Gamble's temper, but how could I? You found out soon enough by yourself, I guess."

The young woman's words were so guileless and disarming, Sylvie found herself laughing too. "You couldn't have said something like that to a stranger on the phone," she agreed.

"Still, had I known the grand finale on the control tower, I might have at least hinted."

"You know about that scene?" Sylvie asked, surprised.

"Are you kidding? I could hear the siren clear up here. The whole seafood plantation, the servants, everybody knows about it. They shrug and say, 'What else can you expect?' Everybody knows Dr. Gamble's temperament."

"Everybody?" Sylvie wondered if that included Steve. Surely the details had been reported to him, blow by blow. Still, he was Virginia's . . . what? Fiancé, husband to be, lover?

Mahina nodded in reply to her question, then she said, "Grandmother told me she gave you her necklace." As Sylvie would learn later, Mahina's conversation often darted from one subject to another like a hummingbird alighting on a variety of flowers seeking nectar.

"I hope you don't mind," Sylvie said. "Did you think it should have stayed in your family?"

Mahina's laughter pealed again as she twirled and her colorful, striped sundress billowed around her long, shapely legs. "Oh, no. Grandmother knew I had an *ipo*—sweetheart—already. His name is Joe. I don't need the necklace." Her eyes sparkled as she saw Sylvie's hand fly to the beads. She laid a gentle hand on Sylvie's shoulder. "It works, you know."

Sylvie stammered, "I wear it because I love it, not to make . . . not because he . . ."

Mahina's young eyes hinted of an ancient wisdom. "Be careful, Sylvie. I tell you because we're going to be friends. The goddess Pele knows your heart better than you do, and her power is great."

"You can't be serious!" Sylvie cried. "I know this is a land of legends, but . . ."

Mahina grinned, sat back at her desk, and resumed her typing. Sylvie retreated to the lab and began wiping off the culture bottles with iodine. Following the instructions, she inoculated the bottles with blood specimens, placed them on the rotator in a vertical position, and continued, step by step, until it was time to place them in the incubator. By then it was lunchtime.

Sylvie and Mahina sat on the veranda while

Muriel, a round, middle-aged woman in a bright orange and yellow mumu, her features typical of the half-Hawaiian, half-Korean people so prevalent in the islands, served them ham sandwiches, sliced pineapple, and cold milk.

The afternoon slipped by as quickly as the morning had, and when it was time for them to go home, Mahina said to Sylvie, "If you bring a bathing suit, we can use part of our lunch hour for a swim once in a while, if you want." She reached into the bottom drawer of her desk and pulled out a wadded purple bikini. "See, I keep mine here, just in case I feel like going for a dip."

"That sounds great!" Sylvie said, thinking how fun it would be here with Mahina, and how different from working with Virginia.

She and Mahina became good friends as they developed the habit of going for a swim every day. Lunchtime usually was the high point of the day, and Sylvie looked forward to the run down the steep path in the cliff to the sliver of beach below. The girls swam and splashed near the shore and dived off the dock that projected in the deeper water. Later, while they ate lunch on the veranda, they dried their hair in the sun. Sylvie loved to sit in the scent-laden air among the flowers and the songs of the birds while she and Mahina chatted about Steve's discovery and the progress of Sylvie's experiments.

After Sylvie had been working at the lab about a week, Mahina called one morning to let her know she wouldn't be in because of a slight indisposition. At lunchtime, Sylvie decided to go swimming by herself. She had just stepped into the water when she heard the roar of a motor. She looked up and saw a white launch rounding the eastern arm of the bay.

Steve, handsome in white slacks and a navy-blue polo shirt, maneuvered the launch alongside the dock and called to her, "Want to go for a short cruise?"

Sylvie, her heart hammering under her red tank suit, ran along the sun-bleached boards of the dock and jumped into the launch, remarking, "I can't stay but a short time. I've some cultures that have to come out of the incubator in less than an hour."

He nodded and replied, "I'll have you back in time. Come over here." He indicated the seat next to his.

As soon as she was at his side, he revved up the motor and the launch shot out toward the open sea, cutting the waves like a flying wedge. Spray flew on each side of the bow like the wings of a gull, and the wind took possession of Sylvie's hair and blew it behind her like golden streamers.

Conversation was impossible above the roar of the motor, so she abandoned herself to the wind, the speed, the spray, the sun, and Steve's silent, compelling presence. But she wondered if he knew of her and Mahina's habit of swimming at this hour. Did he know Mahina was ill today? She tried to tell herself that it didn't matter, but she knew it did.

Behind them, the coast receded. Sylvie saw the cove with the jutting headland, then Kakapuu Lighthouse, Hanauma Bay, Koko Head, Koko Crater, and the ever-present profile of Diamond Head. The mountains formed a backdrop to the angular coastline, and soon the houses looked as small as toys, then were completely lost from view.

Just as she wished this fast ride would last forever, Steve turned the launch in a wide arc and, smiling at her, shouted, "Back to duty, as I promised."

She stood on the dock and watched him speed

away toward Honolulu. The widening wake was the only evidence of his presence that remained in the green waters of the bay.

As time passed, Sylvie became increasingly adept at the laboratory procedures. She was busy each day from the time she arrived at the lab until she returned home, but the pace was leisurely and unhurried, and the results appeared promising. Despite her secret resolve not to let herself think about Steve, Sylvie had to admit to herself that, especially since the unexpected treat of the fast launch ride, whenever two or three days passed without his appearing at the lab on some errand or other, she felt a vague, and sometimes not so vague, sense of loss.

At lunch one day Mahina wore a red hibiscus behind her right ear and a lei of red plumeria. She brought a lei for Sylvie and picked a red hibiscus from a shrub near the veranda, then tucked it behind Sylvie's left ear. "Finish your lunch fast," she directed. "I'm going to give you a hula lesson."

"Oh, no," Sylvie demurred, "I could never learn it. I love the music, but I've never had any training in ballet or anything like that."

"Don't be silly. You're so tiny and graceful, I know it'll come easily to you. The secret is in the hands. Every hula tells its own special story. I'll teach you."

Finally Sylvie let Mahina show her some simple hand movements. Sylvie was so comfortable with Mahina that she felt no self-consciousness as she practiced, to the accompaniment of the gently lapping waves and the high cries of gulls that swooped overhead in the sunlight. There were just the two of them, and Muriel, who hummed old Hawaiian songs and kept time with split-bamboo rattles, to provide an appreciative audience. No other eyes were near; the place was protected by trees, shrubs, and the sea.

"Now, take off your shoes," Mahina said the next day. "I'm your *kumu*—that means teacher—and you're my *haumana*, the pupil. Remember, it's not just the hands that tell a story. Your whole body speaks, from head to feet—the eyes, the hips, everything."

"I don't see how I could think about all those things at once."

"Yes, you can. This is the story of a princess on a wide, lonesome beach." Mahina extended her arms, hands open and palms down. "She's cold, her secret lover is late, so she covers herself with her *ahuula*." Mahina cupped her hands and placed each on the opposite shoulder, as if she were hugging herself, then her hands fell gracefully down to give the impression of the long, feathered robes once worn by Hawaiian royalty. While she moved her hands waved like the fronds of a palm tree in a soft breeze, her feet danced, her knees slightly bent, and her eyes spoke of worry and sorrow, while her hips swayed in a graceful, fluid motion.

Sylvie tried to imitate Mahina as well as she could, while Muriel and Mahina prodded, encouraged, and laughed with delight when finally she was able to coordinate the movements of hands, feet, and body. The facial expressions were more difficult. Although her eyes were supposed to be looking sad and worried, they sparkled and laughed in the midday sun.

"Don't worry, it'll come," Mahina encouraged. "Remember, this is just your second lesson. You're not only supposed to be a dancer, you're also an actress. Unless your eyes look sad, who's going to believe you're worried you'll never see your *ipo* again?"

Sylvie imagined that Steve had married Virginia and moved to Australia. She'd never, never see him again . . .

"Good!" Mahina cried. "Try to remember how you did that. You'll be ready for the luau by Labor Day weekend!"

"What luau? I thought luaus were pretty much for the tourists now."

"The McCloud sugar plantation makes its own traditions," Mahina said firmly. "Our luau is a fifty-year-old tradition, and you must come. We usually have a few guests—corporation staff or customers from the mainland—but mostly the luau is for our own people, and it's like it always has been."

The lunch break was almost over. Facing the sea gulls and the ocean, Sylvie was practicing her pantomime of a desolate beach and a heartbroken, yearning girl, when a spatter of enthusiastic clapping startled her. She turned with a smile for Mahina, her supportive *kumu*, and felt a hot rush of blood leap from her neck to her face until she knew she rivaled the crimson of her hibiscus and her plumeria lei.

Steve stood framed in the sliding glass door, applauding her performance. "You dance as if you'd learned the hula before you learned to walk," he told her. "And what a story those hands tell!"

Sylvie barely wrung a "thank you" from her dry throat and, in one swift motion, slipped on her shoes and fled back to the lab.

She hurried to the microscope and was peering at a slide when she heard Steve ask Mahina if she'd had a chance to transcribe all the letters he'd left for her on three tape cassettes.

"No, Mr. McCloud, two tapes are done and the letters are ready for your signature, but . . ."

"There's no hurry, Mahina. I wanted to see

how things were going in the lab, and I thought if the letters were ready I'd mail them all. But it doesn't matter. I'll sign what you've finished, then I have to fly to the Big Island for the afternoon. You can use my rubber-stamp signature on the rest.''

Mahina went back to her typing and Steve joined Sylvie on the opposite side of a two-headed microscope. They faced each other across the narrow table, each peering down through the eyepieces. Sylvie's hair, which she usually tied back with a ribbon or a scarf while working in the lab, had come free during her hula lesson. Now it fell forward, hiding her face, but when she glanced up over the rim of the eyepiece without raising her head, her eyes met his in a moment of dizzying intensity. She looked back down at the slide. His breath, so close on the other side of the double-headed microscope, made her hair stir slightly, and she was aware of his fresh, spicy cologne. With his right hand he moved the slide to examine another field. His other hand barely touched hers, which lay idle on the small table. She held her breath and stood very still, the stained slide under the scope a blur of blues and reds with no meaning, no purpose. For the most fleeting of moments, his hand lingered on hers as a sea breeze caresses a flower. Then, like one praising an obedient student, he said matter-of-factly, ''Excellent. I'm very satisfied with the progress we're making.''

He was talking about the research, of course. He couldn't be referring to progress in a nonexistent relationship. She wouldn't let herself be so foolish as to imagine that. Yet, his touch hadn't expressed mere approval of her slide-staining technique. It had been more than that, she knew.

The telephone rang on Mahina's desk.

"Sylvie," she called, "it's for you. Long distance."

She hurried to pick up the extension on her small desk in the corner of the lab.

"Hello, darling, this is Fred. How are you?" His exuberant voice boomed from the telephone. "I love the picture you sent me. I keep it on my desk at the office, but when I looked at it today, it made me miss you so much that I couldn't wait to call till you were home."

Sylvie was watching Steve's stiff back. He quickly lowered his head again to the microscope.

"I'm sort of busy right now, Fred, but I'll be home after six for sure, if you want to call then." She knew Steve was listening to every word.

"I don't know how much longer I'll be able to stand being away from you, Syl." Fred's voice was quite clear in the tense atmosphere of the laboratory. "You're too far away. Every night when I get home, I feel like there's something missing."

"Fred . . ."

"I know I promised not to push you about it anymore, but I miss you terribly."

She wanted to cry, "Stop bothering me!" But that wasn't fair. This whole situation wasn't fair to Fred or to herself. She'd have to make a decision, no matter how difficult. "I'll write to you," she told him. "I'll write tonight, I promise."

As she replaced the phone in its cradle, Steve stood up and faced her, his eyes like blue-green ice. He flicked the red hibiscus from her left ear and it lay at her feet like a discarded valentine. "Even flowers lie these days," he shot at her, and then strode away through Mahina's office.

She watched his stiff figure until it receded down the hall and out of sight. He didn't even

seem to hear Mah
didn't sign the letter

"What in the world
the doorway between h

"I don't know," Sylvie
and so did Mahina.

Mahina's dark eyes spark
Imitating a soothsayer's fo
tions, she advanced slowly tov
lifted the green necklace, then le
place while she intoned, "The
goddess Pele is working." She gigg
you, remember?"

"Oh, come on, Mahina. This is serio
really upset."

"Why? Did the phone call upset you . .
much as it did Mr. McCloud?"

Sylvie followed Mahina into her office an
paced restlessly. Not answering Mahina's question directly, she said at last, "I'll have to break
up with Fred."

"It's about time." Mahina's eyes were serious
now.

"What do you mean? I've told you how long
we've gone together and how right we are for
each other in so many ways."

"But you're not in love with him, and that's
the key to everything." Mahina twisted her engagement ring as she spoke, and a quick little
smile showed that she was thinking of Joe.
"That's not something you can will. It's either
there or it isn't. It's as clear as . . . as the lens of
your microscope. You've had plenty of time to
find out, and you must know by now that for
you, the feeling isn't there . . . for Fred, that is.
Isn't it time you faced the truth?"

No, the blaze of love surrounding Sylvie was
not for Fred. At last she admitted it to herself.

Aloha My Love

"Mr. McCloud, you
...na calling.
..."

... ?" Mahina asked from
...er office and the lab.
...replied. "But she knew.

...led with mischief.
...eboding incanta-
...ard Sylvie and
...it fall back in
...spell of the
...ed. "I told
...us. I'm
...as

been
can't
Oh,
dn't

ow
)."
ho
t
a
e
engaged
claimed to be en-

... t the rest of the afternoon in a blur of
...isery and meticulous note-taking. Steve didn't
appear again at the lab, nor had she expected
him to. Back at the carriage house, she didn't
say much during dinner. She was aware of
Debbie's unspoken concern, but she volunteered
no explanation for her silence. She spent a painful hour writing to Fred. Her letter was as warm
as she could make it, but it was firm and left no
hope that there was a chance for them to marry
or return to the old relationship. Friendship was
all she could offer, and not even that for a while.
With no comment, she handed Debbie the letter.

Debbie read it and her eyes filled with tears.
"Poor Fred," she said. "It'll break his heart. Are
you sure this is what you want?"

"You must know, by this time. Don't you
think this is the best way, now that I'm sure I
don't love him?"

Debbie looked at her and stopped crying. "It's Steve McCloud, isn't it?"

"I can't help it. When he's near me it's all I can do to keep from throwing myself at him. I want to follow him into the next room, or to the moon, or wherever he goes. I know he's as good as engaged to Virginia, so I try just to forget all about her. I don't think about anything when I'm with Steve, except wanting to be with him forever."

"If that's the way you really feel about Steve, you're right to break it off with Fred, and I'm proud of you for having the courage to do it. I just hate to think of his being hurt. But you're right, and what you're doing is more honest than what you were doing before."

That night Sylvie slept more soundly than she had since leaving Oklahoma. No restless dreams of a wistful Fred or a painfully polite Steve troubled her. It was as though her store of emotional energy had been used up.

During the next week she began to feel better about Fred. He wrote her a cool, brief letter, accepting her decision. But letters from him soon started appearing in the mailbox at the carriage house, addressed to Debbie. From her roommate's occasional remarks, Sylvie deduced that he was writing to Debbie for news of her. Sylvie wanted Debbie to discourage him in this, but she felt it wasn't her place to say anything about it.

At the lab, Sylvie rarely saw Steve. If he needed to check her work, he went into the lab early in the morning before she arrived, or late in the day after she had left. They communicated mainly through Mahina. He dictated his memos for Sylvie to Mahina, and Sylvie did the same with her messages for him. Occasionally she heard his voice in the office. Once, when she arrived at work a few minutes early, he was dashing down the front steps and barely nodded with a curt "hello." Twice, as she passed the seafood plantation while driving to the lab, she saw his white Jaguar parked beside Virginia's red Porsche beneath the control tower. She purposefully avoided looking toward Virginia's condominium at night. If Steve was there, she didn't want to know.

At work, she and Mahina continued the lunchtime hula lessons on the veranda. "You're making real progress," Mahina told her one day. "This Sunday you'll dance at the luau."

"I couldn't!" She'd been learning for her own amusement, not for a public performance. Besides, Steve probably would be there.

"You will." Mahina's usually gentle voice was determined. "I'm your *kumu,* and I say you're ready. And a *haumana* always obeys her *kumu.* Right?"

Sylvie nodded a doubtful agreement. She was feeling much more confident in her ability to perform the intricate, graceful motions of the ancient dance. Mahina had explained that in early times, the hula served an important purpose in preserving the Hawaiians' traditions, combining poetry, religion, drama, and dance in one undulating blend. Sylvie liked the thought of being part of the long line of nameless dancers who carried on this art form.

"Are you sure there won't be any tourists there?" she asked.

"I've told you before," Mahina replied. "This happens once a year, on Labor Day weekend, at the McCloud sugar plantation. It has become a traditional homecoming for the workers and for those like me, who grew up there and left. We usually have some others who are connected with McCloud Enterprises, but there's no rank that day. We are all *aikanes*— friends—together, united in the spirit of aloha."

Forgetting her shyness about dancing the hula, Sylvie asked, "Would it be all right for me to bring Debbie, if I can persuade her to come? I told her I'd ask, but for some reason she absolutely refuses."

"Of course Debbie is welcome. We'll all have a good time. Tell her we'll leave on the early flight this Sunday, the day of the luau. Why don't you sleep at my place Saturday night, so we can start bright and early? Debbie could still meet us at the commuter plane if she changes her mind."

"I'd love to." Sylvie gave Mahina a quick hug. "I can't believe I'm going to a real luau and not just something like the hotels stage for the tourists, although I know those are fun too."

This was the most exciting thing that had happened in days. Since Sylvie had written her good-bye to Fred, she had been much more comfortable with herself. Although she knew her love for Steve was hopeless, her conscience was at rest about Fred, and she tried not to torment herself with dreams of Steve, the man she could not have. She busied herself with work, and sometimes in the evenings she and Debbie explored ethnic restaurants in the area. Time would mend her heart and dim her memories of the brief moments she and Steve had shared on Kilauea, the evening on the Surf Club terrace when they had danced as one, and the breathless midday cruise in his launch when they had been alone—one with sea, sky, wind, and spray. Soon she would forget the handful of instants at the lab when he had let her know he was aware of her as a woman, rather than just as a young technician who happened to work for him. Even his throwing the red hibiscus to the floor had been better than his present, complete withdrawal. The day he had saved her from drowning in the ocean, before they even knew each other's names, seemed an eternity ago.

Now, thinking of Steve, she told Mahina, "I haven't seen Mr. McCloud for a while and the research project is nearly complete. Did you give him my memo?"

"Oh, yes, I forgot to tell you. He said he'd looked over your notes and your logbook, and everything is great." She giggled softly and whispered, "Jealousy is killing him."

"Mahina! Just because of that phone call from Fred? It doesn't make any sense. You know he's involved with Virginia."

"I wouldn't know about that. Just remember to wear the necklace and everything'll turn out all right, the way it did for my grandmother."

"Please, Mahina, stop the nonsense. Did he leave me a memo or a message?"

"Yes. No, he—"

"Yes or no?"

"Well, he told me the data seemed perfect." Mahina smiled. "He knew I'd tell you he'd said that—'perfect,' that is. On the other hand, he seemed disappointed that all the data wasn't tabulated. . . ."

"He hasn't told me to do that yet!"

"I'm sure he realizes it. But I think he was anxious to send the specifications to his patent attorney before the long Labor Day weekend."

"I can finish the tabulations by . . . noon tomorrow. Please call him and tell him everything'll be ready by then."

"Well, he isn't in Honolulu. He had to leave suddenly for San Francisco and won't be back till Saturday night."

Sylvie felt an overwhelming sense of disappointment at having let him down, even though she knew that it really had been up to him to instruct her, since she had no knowledge of the timetable she was expected to follow. She had waited for him to let her know, and now unwittingly she had displeased him. "I wish I'd known he wanted to apply for the patent immediately."

"We can still do it."

"How?" This was all new to Sylvie, but Mahina seemed confident.

"It's simple. First you check your figures, then you give me the formula and specifications of the process, which I'll type in the proper forms. I'll write the letter to the patent attorney in Washington, D.C., using the rubber stamp of Mr. McCloud's signature. We'll send everything by registered mail. We'll also send photocopies of everything—also by registered mail—to Mr. McCloud at his downtown office. I'll mark it DO NOT OPEN and he'll have the postmark as proof of what time his information was mailed, in case there should be any competition for this particular patent."

It didn't sound simple to Sylvie, but Mahina obviously knew what to do. This afternoon, she would start tabulating the results of the months-long experiments Rosina had conducted with Steve, and her own weeks of careful work, and give them a final check the following morning. Then she would write out the specifications for Mahina to type and they'd get the patent application under way.

Nine

By two o'clock Friday afternoon, Mahina had everything neatly typed, and after Sylvie had proofread the letter addressed to the patent attorney, the young Hawaiian woman rubber-stamped Steve's signature to it. Mahina made photocopies for her file and another set to be mailed to Steve's downtown office. She left her copies on her desk, atop a stack of other papers to be filed.

"I can't believe we got it all done!" Sylvie said as they relaxed in wicker chairs on the veranda, drinking iced tea. Watching two sail boats racing toward Kakapuu Lighthouse, she thought of her short cruise with Steve, of the thrill of wind and water as she sat at his side. Then she pushed away the heartache that came with the memory.

"I knew we could," said Mahina, just as Muriel brought them sandwiches and fruit salad. They had worked straight through without stopping for lunch. "Mr. McCloud'll be so pleased we're getting everything mailed today."

"Are you sure? I still feel strange about sending it without his okay."

"There's nothing to worry about—not if your figures are correct and the process really works."

"It works all right. And Mr. McCloud knows it does."

"Fine, then let's go to the post office now. You'd be surprised how important the timing can be on something like this."

"You go on, I'll stay here."

"What for? You don't have a new project started, do you?"

"No, but I want to wipe off all the lab instruments and run some tests on the distilled water. Besides, I haven't put in my full eight-hour day."

Mahina laughed. "Don't worry, you'll make it up, and more. When Mr. McCloud starts a new project, there'll be days when you work ten to twelve hours. Some weekends, too. Anyway, Mr. McCloud won't mind. All I have to do is switch the phone over to take messages."

"All right," Sylvie agreed, "if you're sure it's not a mistake for me to leave early. You know him better than I do."

"Are you sure about that?" Mahina ducked as Sylvie pretended to throw an ice cube at her, then she ran, laughing, back to her office to get the papers.

As the Toyota started down the long, shaded drive, Virginia's Porsche came into sight around a curve. Sylvie pulled wide on the narrow drive and let her pass. With a single impatient honk, Virginia flashed by them in a red blur, staring straight ahead and ignoring Mahina's wave of greeting.

"What was that all about?" asked Sylvie. "Do you think she needs something at the lab?"

"No, she's just bringing up the time cards. She has a key and can leave them on my desk. I don't do payroll till Wednesday, anyway."

"I thought you were supposed to go after the time cards." Sylvie remembered how grateful she had been to Mahina for taking on the job after she had started working at the research lab. It had been a favor, just so she wouldn't have to face Virginia.

"I told her I wouldn't have time today. What we're doing is more urgent. If she needs anything, she can wait till Tuesday," Mahina said. "Or she can talk to me on the Big Island, if she wants to. She's sure to be at the luau."

"Oh," was all Sylvie could respond to this unwelcome news.

"Don't worry, there'll be so many people around, you might not even run into her. And if you do, so what? She's not your boss anymore. She can't do anything to you."

Sylvie wasn't afraid of Virginia. It was just that she had visualized the luau as a happy, festive occasion. There would be laughter and music and delicious food, and the fragrance of hundreds of flowers in the women's leis. She would get to dance the hula, which she had practiced so faithfully with Mahina these past two weeks. Sylvie's earlier misgivings about performing had vanished when she became more accustomed to the graceful gestures, and she was eager to dance to the music of steel guitars and ukuleles instead of Muriel's off-key renditions. She imagined Steve's expression of surprise and delight when he saw her swaying among the other dancers with her ti-leaf skirt and a crown of flowers. She would smile at him while her hands wove their message of love, and he . . .

What nonsense! Now that she knew Virginia would be there, clinging to Steve, Sylvie lost all interest in taking part in the hula. But she didn't want to disappoint Mahina, who had spent so much effort coaching her, so she decided to follow Mahina's advice and try to forget about Virginia.

After they left the post office, Sylvie drove Mahina home and promised to be there the next evening, ready to leave for the Big Island early Sunday morning as planned. Back at the carriage house, she found Debbie sitting outside on the top step, tearing a leaf from the jade vine into tiny pieces and dropping them to the ground one at a time as if this were a very important task she had been assigned.

"Debbie?" Sylvie sat down beside her and put an arm around her shoulders. "What *is* it?"

"I might as well tell you." Debbie jumped up and leaned against the railing, not looking at Sylvie. "It's Fred."

"What about him?" Sylvie had been so engrossed in her new work and her own emotional turmoil about Steve, Fred's name sounded almost like a foreign language.

"He's coming to Honolulu Sunday morning."

"What for? How could you let him?" Sylvie was angry—at Debbie, at herself for her impatience, and at Fred for this intrusion. He would be throwing away his plane fare as well as wasting his time.

"I think he wants to see you." Debbie's voice was barely audible. "I told him you'd be out of town, but you know how persistent he is. And, Syl, I want to see him, even if he doesn't really notice me."

"But, Debbie, is that fair—to let him come all this way when you know I won't be here?"

"He knows you'll be gone. I've already told him."

"You should have been firmer about it."

Sylvie heard the edge in her voice and added, "I'm sorry, Deb. I know it's not your doing."

"Well," Debbie said, "I'll talk to him and . . . would you mind if I brought him to the luau? Wouldn't it be all right, since you've been inviting me to come?"

Sylvie thought for a moment. She was torn between wanting to have Debbie at the celebration and not wanting to see Fred. Although she had been very clear in her letter, apparently he thought she might change her mind. But perhaps when he saw the two roommates together, he would realize how firm Sylvie was in her refusal and how much Debbie cared for him. Too, she felt it her duty to see Fred and make him understand that there was no chance for their relationship. Then he would be free to notice the love that glowed in Debbie's face. "You do whatever you think is best," she said.

Debbie brightened. "What I thought I'd do is bring him here for lunch, talk awhile, then catch an afternoon or evening flight to Hilo. We could rent a car and come just in time for the feast and the dancing."

Sylvie looked at Debbie's shining eyes and the soft curve of her mouth, then hugged her. "Good luck, Deb. I mean that with all my heart."

They went out for pizza that night and spent most of Saturday sprucing up the carriage house for Fred's arrival. Sylvie packed her overnight bag, since Mahina had arranged for her and Sylvie to sleep at her grandmother's cottage after the luau. Sylvie looked forward to seeing Iolani again. She hoped the old woman wouldn't ask how the necklace was working, for she would have to report it had cast no spell at all. Then she thought how ridiculous it was for her to have such thoughts. She had never been superstitious and didn't intend to start now. She fingered the green stones of the necklace which she wore so often that she had begun to feel undressed without it. Somehow, its weight around her neck gave a vague comfort to her fading hopes.

Debbie was scheduled to work Sunday afternoon, but because of Fred's arrival she traded days with another technician at the hospital. When she left for the late shift, she assured Sylvie that she would see her the next day at the luau.

Late that afternoon, as Sylvie was taking a nap on the sofa, the telephone rang. Without getting up, she reached for the phone on the end table and said a drowsy "hello."

"What was our agreement?" Steve's voice was like an icy blade.

"Our what? What agreement?" Sylvie sat up and shook her head, trying to wake up.

"You know very well what agreement!" he barked. "About confidentiality."

"I don't—"

Not giving her a chance to reply, he shouted, "Is there no one I can trust? Have you seen the evening paper? I'm so angry I can't even stand the sound of your voice." He slammed down the receiver.

Stunned, Sylvie sat staring at the telephone, which emitted a plaintive dial tone. She had no idea what he was talking about, but it was obvious that he'd returned from San Francisco and was furious with her.

The evening edition of the *Star Bulletin* lay on the coffee table. She picked it up, turned on a reading lamp, and, not knowing what she was looking for, began scanning the pages. She could find nothing to justify Steve's outburst, yet she was so shaken by his unexplained accusation that she thought perhaps she had missed something. With shaking hands, she leafed through the newspaper again, her eyes going carefully down each column of every page.

There it was, with the business news—a small item at the bottom of the page. She had missed it before, but now it glared at her like a neon sign. DHS REGISTERS ANOTHER FIRST read the small-print headline. Then, in rather vague terms, the story outlined a discovery made by Diamond Head Scientific Corporation. It sounded just like Steve's, and some of the terms in the two short paragraphs were identical to those Sylvie and Mahina had mailed to Washington, D.C., the previous afternoon. Sylvie shook her head in disbelief. It was impossible! She and Mahina were the only two who had access to the information. Not even Steve had known the precise wording of the product description, for he had been in San Francisco when it was prepared and mailed.

Although there were only so many words that could be used to describe a particular scientific discovery, there was no way that this could have been a coincidence. Someone must have taken the file copy from Mahina's desk. Like a flash of fire, she remembered seeing Virginia's red Porsche speeding toward Steve's house just as she and Mahina were leaving for the post office.

Sylvie looked out the window toward Virginia's condominium. It couldn't be! Virginia had her faults—plenty of them—but for her to steal from the man she hoped to marry would be too despicable. But Virginia was the only person who would know what to look for and understand what it meant.

She'd do anything . . . anything . . . anything, Debbie's words echoed in Sylvie's memory.

No. Virginia was too smart to jeopardize her

career, in fact her entire life's work and her future with Steve, just for money. Virginia might be ruthless, but she wasn't stupid. And she claimed to love Steve. What kind of woman would double-cross the man she loved?

Trying to find a clue to what had happened, Sylvie read the newspaper story again and again. There it was, an inexorable fact. Virginia must have thought that Mahina wouldn't mail the material until Steve returned from San Francisco and approved it. She might have stolen the information by making a photocopy of Mahina's file copy, then rushed to Diamond Head Scientific, or even called and dictated it to them from Mahina's office. The larger rival laboratory had the legal staff to take over from there. Their public-relations people would then have contacted the newspaper with their announcement.

This was too farfetched. Sylvie knew there must be some other explanation. She squeezed back tears while she nervously clenched and unclenched her hands. Steve would never know how much his accusation had hurt her. He had allowed her no explanation. He hadn't even given her a chance to tell him that his own patent specifications had been sent off before Diamond Head Scientific could possibly have mailed theirs. The earlier postmark on the duplicate registered letter that she and Mahina had mailed to his downtown office would prove her innocence.

She expelled her breath slowly. Steve's discovery was safe. She was glad of that, even though he'd had no right to doubt her discretion. She had been absolutely trustworthy. Never had she even hinted to Debbie, her closest friend, about the nature of the research project. Virginia, on the other hand, must have been stealing his information at the very moment that Sylvie and Mahina were at the post office, protecting his interests. Diamond Head Scientific had moved fast, but not fast enough.

Sylvie wouldn't tell Steve that she suspected Virginia. His lack of trust in her had destroyed the strong emotions she'd felt for him. She just wanted to let him know his patent was safe, then forget about the entire muddle. She dialed his home number, but there was no answer. She dialed the lab, only to have Mahina's recorder tell her to leave a message. His car wasn't parked at Virginia's. She started getting ready to spend the night at Mahina's, since she couldn't find Steve.

She showered, then put on the coral dress she'd worn the first time she'd seen Steve, in front of the employment office. His impatience with her that afternoon was nothing in comparison with his present fury. As she slipped the green necklace over her head and brushed her long hair to a golden sheen, she tried to think of some way to reach him. She couldn't go off on a carefree weekend knowing that he still thought she had betrayed him. She kept trying his number, but there was no answer. Perhaps, in his outrage, he had unplugged his phone and didn't want to talk to anyone tonight.

Well, he was going to talk to her!

Hardly aware of what she was doing, she turned out the lights, rushed down to her car, and backed out of the driveway. The landlady called to her from her back porch, but Sylvie was in a hurry, so she pretended she hadn't seen or heard her. Right now, she had to get to Steve's house. This ugly thing must not be left hanging between them, nor did she want it to spoil her first luau tomorrow. If he thought his months of work had gone for nothing, he might not even show up at the luau. It was urgent that she tell him his discovery was safe.

Gravel spurted when she turned off the highway and onto the narrow road to the seafood plantation. The control tower gleamed in the moonlight, and a faint blue light from the computer panel reflected on the glass.

Sylvie slowed her car for the curve leading to the front of Steve's sprawling home, then sharply applied the brakes when she saw what awaited her there. Virginia's red Porsche was parked in the circular driveway. Such an avalanche of fury engulfed her that her hands began to shake on the steering wheel and her knuckles turned white. This was more than she could handle. With a squeal of tires, she sped around the drive, not caring whether she disturbed them in their cozy nest. No wonder he hadn't answered his telephone! He didn't want to be interrupted. Right now they were probably sitting on the veranda, having cocktails and watching the surf break on the cove below. Or perhaps they were having a candlelight dinner, with the flames reflected in their eyes.

It wasn't fair for that creature to get away with selling Steve out and having him too. Sylvie knew there must be a way to prove that what she suspected was true. The evidence had to be somewhere. Virginia wouldn't risk leaving anything incriminating at Wai Huihui, for Steve sometimes stopped there on his way to the lab. Virginia's home was the only possible place.

A mad idea swirled amid the chaotic blend of hurt and indignation in Sylvie's mind. Did she dare? Virginia was back there at Steve's and almost surely would be there for some time. Probably she was consoling him for Sylvie's supposed betrayal. Grandma Brooke's words echoed in her mind: *Who laughs last, laughs best.* Virginia was surely laughing at Sylvie now, but not for long! If Sylvie's suspicions were true, any proof that existed would be in Virginia's condominium. It would take Sylvie just a few minutes to slip in from the lanai and search for . . . for what?

How could she even consider breaking into Virginia's home when she had no proof of any wrongdoing? But proof was what she needed. Proof that would show Steve what Virginia was really like and would keep him from making the mistake of a lifetime. For Steve's sake, she decided to do it—do it right now, before Virginia returned.

Sylvie parked her Toyota in front of the carriage house and sat there, stunned by the enormity of what she was about to attempt. There was no time to waste, no time to plan, to regret, to lose her resolve. The reserved, reticent young woman who'd left Oklahoma such a short time ago had learned what was important to her and how to fight for it. She was fighting right now, fighting for the respect of the man she loved.

Knowing that she'd have to hurry, Sylvie opened the car door, then rushed down the path behind the carriage house. A rustle in the bushes made Sylvie's heart skip a beat, then trip on at a mad pace. Hidden among the shrubbery, she hardly dared to breathe. A white blur streaked by her feet, darted behind the carriage house, and disappeared. It was only a cat.

Sylvie took a deep breath to steady herself before climbing over the low wall surrounding the lanai. The light was dim. There was just a half-moon in the starlit sky, and only a faint glimmer from a streetlight reached the lanai. Nevertheless, Sylvie felt as exposed as if a spotlight were trained on her as she tiptoed forward, listening to the voices, laughter, and soft music coming from another condominium. A car approached and she held her breath, poised for flight, but the car moved on.

She reached the sliding glass doors and pulled the handle. She hadn't considered that of course Virginia's doors would be locked. In bitter frustration, Sylvie pushed, pulled, and shook the doors, but they didn't budge. Next, she tried the three windows at the back of the condominium. They too were locked. She didn't dare try the front door or the windows at the sides and front of the place, for surely someone would see her. But she wasn't going to give up. Not yet. She retraced her steps to her car and opened the trunk, not knowing what tool she hoped to find. She rebelled at the thought of using the jack to break the sliding glass doors. Then suddenly she stopped. How could she even entertain such a thought? She imagined neighbors calling the police, sirens screaming, and being arrested. Quietly she closed the trunk, wondering what she could use to trip the lock on the glass doors. Then she remembered that once, as a child, she had accidentally locked herself out of her home and a bobby pin had done the trick.

Like a cat riffling a sewing basket, she dug through the accumulation of necessities and junk that filled her purse. She knew there was a bobby pin somewhere in the deep reaches of her handbag, because she'd been using it to pin the hibiscus behind her ear as she learned to dance the hula. Finally, she found it.

She threw her purse back into the car and, with the bobby pin clutched in her hand, hurried back to the sliding glass doors. Time was quickly running out as she inserted the pin, pushed, pried, jiggled, and lifted the door a tiny fraction. There was a click, then the lock snapped. The door slid open and Sylvie entered Virginia's domain.

The faint light filtering through from the lanai guided her to a lamp, which she turned on after closing the raw-silk drapes. She caught her breath at the luxurious room. Almost everything was eggshell white, a perfect foil for Virginia's ivory skin and dark hair. The thick carpet matched the walls and drapes, velvet sofas flanked an enormous fireplace, and overhead was a cathedral ceiling of strikingly beautiful wood. Between the sofas was a smoked-glass coffee table on a zebra skin. Sylvie's urgent gaze swept all this in her frantic search for a desk, a drawer, a pile of papers. The room was spotless and uncluttered. There was no hiding place.

Sylvie hurriedly searched an equally uncluttered dining room furnished in polished pecan with a lighted glass cabinet that displayed fine china. The marble counters of the kitchen beyond were bare. Sylvie found Virginia's bedroom done in pale greens like the jungle lair of a tigress. Virginia's subtle, musky perfume scented the room with warning. At any moment, she might return.

An elaborate Chinese screen stood in the corner between the flowered chaise and the antique lacquered desk. There, at last, a desk! Her heart thudding, Sylvie ran to it and leaned over to examine some papers piled neatly behind an ornate brass lamp. As she bent, her necklace caught on a prong of the lamp and the green beads scattered on the desk and bounced off, losing themselves in the silence of the plush carpet.

Sylvie dropped to her hands and knees and began searching through the plush carpet. When she'd gathered up all the beads, she reached for an envelope atop the papers on the desk, planning to put them in it. She gasped upon seeing that, although the envelope was empty and bore no address, the printed return address was that of Diamond Head Scientific.

Be calm, a mere empty envelope is no proof, she thought. Still, her suspicions had been vindicated, and she sat down at the desk to continue her search with renewed vigor. A corner of pale green paper sticking out from beneath the broad base of the lamp caught her eye, and she pulled it out. It was the stub of a check for twenty thousand dollars from Diamond Head Scientific. It bore today's date.

She sat there holding the check stub that would exonerate her and incriminate Virginia. Then suddenly she noticed that beside the desk was a leather wastebasket filled with crumpled pieces of paper. She unfolded one of them. It was a photocopy of the first page of the specifications that she and Mahina had prepared so carefully the day before. She didn't have to look any further.

Sylvie gathered the rest of the papers from the wastebasket, smoothed them flat, folded them, and put the check stub in the envelope with her beads. Turning off the lights as she went, she swiftly retraced her steps, feeling disgusted at Virginia's lack of integrity. Sylvie ran through the living room and out to the lanai, closing the glass doors behind her. Threading her way among the wrought-iron furniture outside, she climbed back over the wall and returned to her own driveway. The sounds of traffic and night birds seemed very distant, and she felt encased in a silent, airless bubble.

Sylvie made a quick decision. She would go back to Steve's and confront the two of them with her proof. Her knees weak from her ordeal, she got into the Toyota, stuffed the envelope and the papers into her purse, and took off. When she furnished the proof, Virginia could try her own explaining, but surely Steve would see through any excuses she might concoct. But what was most important of all was that Steve would know she hadn't betrayed him.

A little doubt gnawed in a hidden corner of Sylvie's mind as she drove along the familiar route. Was her concern only for her reputation and for Steve's potential loss of income? Wasn't it also that she couldn't stand the idea of Virginia becoming Steve's wife if he didn't learn the truth?

As she neared Steve's house, her dread of facing Virginia increased, as did her indignation at being falsely accused by the man with whom she had fallen in love. But now she wondered how she could love a man who could think she would betray him. Until this moment, it had not occurred to Sylvie that although he had held himself aloof from her because she was his employee, he was involved with Virginia, who was also his employee. It wasn't fair. But he had stopped being fair to her long ago. His accusation tonight was the supreme example.

She braked to a jolting stop before Steve's house. Virginia's Porsche was gone. But it was Steve she was angry with now. She had succeeded in covering her hurt with her anger. She raced across the veranda and, without knocking, ran to the living room. Her heels tapped an insistent staccato on the tiled floor.

Steve was sitting by the French windows sipping from a brandy snifter and watching the play of the moon over the waves in the cove below. He turned as she entered, then rose to meet her, his expression guarded and cold.

Breathless and chilled, although the night was warm, Sylvie glared at him from the doorway.

Without saying a word, she reached into her purse, yanked out the papers and check stub, and flung them at him. They fluttered to the pale carpet like scraps of trash in a gust of wind. "There's your proof that I'm not the one who forgot her 'arrangement' with you!" She flung the words after the papers. "The check stub from Diamond Head Scientific was in Virginia's bedroom, and so was a photocopy of the patent specifications that Mahina and I sent off to you and your attorney by registered mail yesterday afternoon!" She wheeled around and ran from the room.

As she descended the steps of the veranda, she heard his quick step behind her in the entry hall, but she didn't wait for him. Nothing he could say or do would soothe the hurt that enveloped her. Trust was the cornerstone of love—without trust, there was nothing. Feeling cold and empty, she jumped into her car and sped out of the McCloud domain.

She became a little calmer on the way home. Not rushing as she had when driving out, she watched the moon silvering the waves. When she reached the driveway, she saw a light shining through the carriage house window. It was too early for Debbie's shift at the hospital to be over, and Sylvie was sure she had turned off the lamp when she'd left. Hoping nothing was wrong, she pushed open the door.

"What did you do with it?" Virginia, in a black cocktail dress, stood in the middle of the living room, with papers scattered on the floor all around her.

Still in the doorway, Sylvie raised her chin and replied, "You won't find either the check stub or the copies of the patent specifications, Dr. Gamble. Your employer has them, and it shouldn't take him long to figure out what they mean."

Virginia lunged at Sylvie and grabbed a handful of her hair. "You lying little schemer!" she shouted. "Don't you know he'll believe me, not you?"

Sylvie grasped the other woman's wrist and freed her hair from the frenzied grip. "Dr. Gamble, don't ever do that again," she warned, "and if you don't want me to call the police, you'd better leave right now."

Virginia reached into her pocket, thrust a clenched fist under Sylvie's nose, then opened her hand. In her palm lay one of the green stones from Sylvie's broken necklace. "Call the police, indeed," she spat. "I found this bead of yours in *my* wastebasket, beside *my* desk, in *my* bedroom. I'm the one who'll be calling the police on you, for breaking and entering."

Sylvie snatched the bead out of Virginia's hand and grabbed the suitcases she had left by the door just a few hours before. This had been the longest evening of her life. Running down to her car, she called behind her, "You do that, Virginia. Just go right ahead."

Ten

Joe Lahine picked up Sylvie and Mahina at the Hilo airport. Mahina's fiancé, who was the foreman at the McCloud sugar mill, was a huge man with the strong features of his pure-blooded Hawaiian ancestors. He had smiling eyes that seemed to peer into the distance, expecting good things to happen.

"Who's this you've brought, a *haole* mermaid with flowing hair made from the light of sunrise?" he teased Mahina.

"This is Sylvie. You know, I wrote you all about her." Mahina smiled. "Isn't she even prettier than I said?" Her eyes signaled Sylvie. "You see why I love him so much?" she whispered.

Joe helped Sylvie into the back seat of his jeep. During the drive to the sugar plantation, he and Mahina kept up a continual stream of laughter and talk, while Sylvie rode behind with her troubled thoughts.

After the trauma of last night's events, she

was trying to sort out her feelings so that she could enter into the spirit of the luau. She wasn't concerned about Virginia's threat to have her arrested for breaking into the condo, for Virginia would then face the counter-threat of being charged with entering the carriage house, not to mention the business about the patent. She wondered what Steve thought about his inamorata now, having examined the evidence Sylvie had provided. She wished that she had calmly handed him the papers, but throwing them at him had provided a much-needed emotional release.

"What's the big frown about?" Joe asked over his shoulder, when his glance happened to meet Sylvie's in the rear-view mirror. "Only smiles are allowed at luau time."

"Nothing's wrong. I'm just tired," Sylvie lied.

"Okay," he said cheerfully. "Just remember, you have come to a good place. Mahina and I, we want everyone to have good aloha, like us. We'll help you forget your troubles."

"I'll count on that." Sylvie produced a wan smile. She didn't want to be a damper on Mahina's reunion with her exuberant fiancé on this day of celebration.

She looked ahead of them to Mauna Kea, the dormant volcano shrouded in morning mist, forming a backdrop to Hilo. Her thoughts skittered to Kilauea and the Halemaumau fire pit, where Steve's embraces and his kisses had awakened in her the knowledge of what love could mean, a kind of love she had not even imagined.

It all seemed so long ago, and it had led only to heartache and disappointment for herself, for Fred, and . . . no, not for Steve. To him, it had been just a mild flirtation, an exercise in masculine power. Her only value to him was as an employee.

She felt foolish for having allowed herself to fall in love with him. The weeks of hoping, longing—what a waste of time and emotion. She felt like going to Kilauea and telling the mythical goddess of the volcano what she thought of her heartless jokes.

They drove between tall green walls of sugar cane as she and Steve had done in July, but today there were no workers in the field. The field of vanda orchids was deserted also, and as they began to climb uphill along the avenue of ohia trees, Sylvie heard voices and music from afar.

Smiling with excitement, Mahina said, "I look forward to this all year. As I told you, it's my homecoming."

With a twinge of nostalgia, Sylvie remembered her first homecoming day when she was a freshman at the University of Oklahoma. She had just met Fred and could tell that he liked her, and as she sat in the stands and joined in the frenzied cheering when Fred scored a touchdown, she'd thought she would explode with pride and joy. But right now the thought of seeing Fred again was an added worry. She thought how eager and trusting she had been during her college days. Yet, in one short summer on her own, she had learned enough of intrigue and betrayal—and love glimpsed, love lost—to last the rest of her life. Someday, perhaps, she would stop crying inside.

"Look, Sylvie, there's the old Stewart place," Mahina said, pointing to a two-story frame house surrounded by trees, just a mile downhill from the McCloud estate. "Six more months and Joe and I'll have enough money saved to buy it. There are five acres planted in macadamia nuts and four acres in papayas. That'll help with our finances when I stop working full time. Old Mr. Stewart is going to move to Maui and live with his daughter, as soon as we have the money.''

"It's lovely. How lucky you are to have it available at the right time,'' Sylvie said, wishing she could be more like Mahina, who knew what she wanted and put herself in the right position to make it happen. No wonder Iolani hadn't offered her granddaughter the green necklace! Mahina didn't need it. She didn't vacillate between marrying Joe and developing a career, and she didn't dissipate her love on someone she couldn't have.

"Oh, he could have sold the farm a long time ago,'' Mahina said. "He's sticking to his agreement with us because he likes to help young people get ahead, and he likes Joe. Everybody likes my Joe.''

"Six more months is a long time. Isn't it hard to wait?'' Sylvie asked. Steve hadn't even waited for her to explain about the patent before he hung up on her.

"Six months isn't too long when we think of the rest of our lives together,'' Mahina said quickly.

Joe's arm encircled his fiancée's shoulder, and with a light squeeze of his powerful hand he said, "Then you'll move back to the Big Island, where you belong, with me.''

Now they had skirted the McCloud mansion and were driving along a small road at the back of the estate. The joyful sounds of singing and laughter grew louder. On a vast green stretch of meadow, with a magnificent view of rolling fields and the deep-blue ocean in the distance, several hundred people were milling about. Scantily clad children ran among the brightly dressed adults, all of whom wore leis. The grown-ups sat in folding chairs or on blankets, or walked around trying to talk to everyone at once, or lolled in the grass, all the while laughing and singing. Young men strummed love songs, and babies cried, only to be shushed by their mothers or handed to older sisters. There was constant movement among the crowd, a current of coming and going as of bees in a clover field. Mingling with the perfume of the leis was the tantalizing aroma of the pigs, that had been roasting since dawn in underground ovens.

Long tables were laden with food, and new arrivals added their own delicacies, all of which were greeted by exclamations of joy. As Joe drove slowly by this area, many of the revelers greeted him and Mahina with shouts or enthusiastic waves.

They turned into Iolani's drive and Sylvie saw the old woman standing on her small front porch, her ear turned toward the jeep. She wore a brightly flowered mumu and her wizened face looked happy and serene.

"I'll see you later, Granny," Joe called to her. He gave Mahina a quick kiss and said, "I'd better go help at the *imus.* I'll see you both later." Then he hurried toward the underground ovens.

"Come on, Syl, let's go see Grandmother." Mahina ran to hug and kiss Iolani. The opaque, sightless eyes held a peaceful contentment as Iolani caressed Mahina's face, tracing her features. She smiled serenely, then turned to Sylvie, who was waiting on the walk beside the border of sweet alyssum. Not one weed marred the perfection of the flowers. Iolani could garden with her sense of touch.

"Come, child, let me greet you." Iolani extended her arms and Sylvie went into them, her

low spirits responding to a warmth that made
her feel like another beloved granddaughter who
had come home.

"I'm glad to see you again, Iolani," she said. "I
was looking forward to it."

"I, too." Iolani caressed Sylvie's hair, then her
fingers softly outlined the irregularly shaped
green stones of the necklace, which Mahina had
restrung for Sylvie the night before.

As sure of foot as if she could see every step,
Iolani hastened into her house, pulling Sylvie by
the hand. With the ghost of a smile playing
around the corners of her mouth, she shook her
head in pretended concern and said, "Mahina
tells me the necklace has been a disappointment
to you."

"Oh, no, I just love it," Sylvie protested. "I
wear it everywhere, as you can see."

"I see, indeed. I see with my heart."

"Oh, Iolani, I have so much to learn from
you." Sylvie hugged her again. "The necklace
reminds me of you, and the day I met you, the
day we went . . ."

She stopped herself short and sat quietly
in the spotless room with its wicker furniture
and a few antique pieces. The room reminded
her of a Polynesian version of the cottage of
the seven dwarfs. In a corner, a carved Hawaiian idol reigned over pots of begonias,
and an old round oak table stood on a braided
rug in the middle of the room. Sylvie found
herself walking a taut string of control today,
maintaining a pretense of happiness to hide the
pain she felt.

"Don't give up yet, child." Iolani's gentle chid-
ing could have been in earnest or in jest; her soft
smile gave no hint. Feeling Sylvie's body stiffen,
the old woman chuckled and said, "I know you
don't believe in the power of the necklace. Who

can tell? Maybe it's just one's imagination that makes it work. It worked for me. And I know that whether you wear it or not, it will also bring you luck." With a sharp clap of her hands, like a queen directing a lady-in-waiting, she said, "Off with you, now. Get that granddaughter of mine and we'll go to the celebration."

In the bedroom they were to share, Sylvie found that Mahina had already changed into a bright red skirt and yellow blouse. Sylvie changed into a dainty ruffled skirt made from wide bands of cotton gauze in contrasting colors, and a peasant-style blouse with pastel embroidery.

The three of them then headed for the group scattered on the grassy slope, Mahina carrying a folding chair for her grandmother, and Iolani, who trotted along with a surprisingly light step, gripping Sylvie's arm and carrying a cane. When the chair was installed among a group of elderly women who greeted Iolani joyfully, she shooed the girls away, assuring them that she would be all right. "Go on now, both of you, and enjoy yourselves with the other young folks," she said with a wave and a contented smile. "If I get tired, someone else can see me home."

The mouth-watering aroma of roasting pigs flavored the air, the cane fields unfurled in several directions, and the restless sea in the distance embraced the shore. Sylvie felt her depression slipping away.

Three of the men attending the underground ovens were clothed in *lavalavas*—long, skirtlike garments patterned in bold prints. Red plumeria leis hung around their necks and over their massive, bare chests. Joe Lahine's bulk and features seemed to demand that he also wear a *lavalava,* but he was perfectly content with the slacks and crewneck shirt he had worn to the Hilo airport,

now that he had added a lei of vanda orchids to
his conventional outfit.

The costumes of those awaiting the feast included brightly flowered mumus, slacks, jeans,
and sports clothes of every description, but
everyone wore a lei of plumerias or vanda orchids. All the women, young and old, had flowers in their hair, some on the right side and
some on the left. Mahina ran to a hibiscus bush
and picked two red blossoms, one for herself and
one for Sylvie. As the girls pinned the flowers in
place, Mahina's behind her right ear because she
was engaged and Sylvie's behind her left to
show that she was unattached, Sylvie realized
how comfortable and at ease she felt among
these friendly, smiling strangers who, with the
language of flowers, so boldly declared their
emotions. The hula here with them would be as
easy as dancing beside Mahina on Steve's veranda.

Mahina introduced her to what seemed a
countless number of people who worked for
McCloud Enterprises. There were field workers
and typists, cleaning women and executives,
salesmen, technicians, production and advertis-
ing personnel—all from the McCloud empire,
and all of differing ethnic backgrounds. Polynesian, Japanese, Korean, Chinese, Caucasian,
and Filipino—their faces and builds ran the
gamut of all the mixtures of races on the islands.
A happy, carefree atmosphere pervaded the air.

As time for the feast approached, there came
over the group an impalpable electricity, an unspoken awareness of what was about to happen.
The long tables were decorated with birds-of-
paradise, jacarandas, and orchids. The center-
pieces were pyramids of coconuts, mangoes, ba-
nanas, papayas, and pineapples, in beautiful,
exotic arrangements. Shadows were length-

ening across the grassy slope, and soon the
roasting pigs would be dug out of the hot sand
pits.

During the past several hours, Sylvie had
really entered into the spirit of the festivities,
laughing and joking happily with the merry-
makers. Looking forward to the meal, she
glanced at the crowd on the other side of the
imus and, with a sinking heart, saw that the person waving to her was Fred. His face became one
big grin when he saw that she had noticed him.
Debbie was beside him. Reluctantly, she made
her way through the crowd to join her roommate
and her . . . she didn't know what to call Fred.

"Hello, Sylvie, how are you?"

"Just fine, Fred, and you?" The exchange was
superficial, and the strain between them
hummed like a high-tension cable. His face
looked drawn and there was a crease between
his eyebrows that hadn't been there before.

"What a spread!" Debbie offered with an as-
sumed cheerfulness. "It makes me famished
just to look at it." Then she backed away, calling, "I want to just wander around and watch
everything. I'll see you in a little while."

Fred nodded. He couldn't seem to take his
eyes off Sylvie. She glanced away. This was
going to be far more difficult than she had anticipated. "Let's walk where it's quiet," she said
finally.

He followed her toward Iolani's, skirted the
cottage, and strolled on the wide expanse of
lawn that separated the cottage from the
McCloud plantation house.

Fred blurted, "I feel as if I'm making a nui-
sance of myself, Syl. But I couldn't give up till I
heard from your own lips that we're
through. . . ." Sylvie started to speak, but he si-
lenced her with a tired gesture. "No, let me fin-

ish. You know I love you. I guess I have ever since I first saw you that time in the library, a freshman looking so pretty with your hair shining under the light, and so lost. I just have to know, see it in your face, if you're sure you don't want to give us a chance. I suppose it's all my fault. If I hadn't kept after you about getting married right after you graduated, you might not have felt cornered and things would still be the way they were. You might never even have left Oklahoma.''

"Dear, dear Fred." Sylvie reached for his arm and he covered her hand with his. She left her hand in place, his providing a measure of comfort for her unhappiness about Steve. "Don't blame yourself. It's nothing you did," she said. "I know this will hurt, but when you think over what I'm going to say, it may help, too."

"Nothing will help unless I have you, Sylvie." He stared down at his feet.

"Fred, I don't love you," she said softly. "It's simple. I can't marry without love, and you deserve love that I can't give you. I like you so much . . . but as a friend, Fred, as a friend. Not as a lover or a husband."

"I don't care, Syl. I'm willing to wait. In time, you'll learn to love me. If you just give me the chance."

Sylvie couldn't stand it any longer. "Stop this! It makes me cringe! I don't want to remember you like this. But when you're through feeling sorry for yourself, you'll realize it's for the best."

He shook his head in mute denial of everything she had said.

She had to get through to him somehow. "Fred Barton," she exploded, "you're so involved with your own feelings, you can't even see how much you *are* loved!"

"You do love me then, after all?" His face

brightened and he swung her around, his hands clutching her arms.

"No, no, no!" She stamped her foot on the grass. "Not the way you mean! Are you blind? Don't you see that Debbie's the one who loves you the way you want to be loved? The way I can't love you! She's been in love with you for years, with all the commitment and warmth and sureness you want from me."

Fred shook his head. "Debbie's great and I'd do anything for her, but she's just a good friend."

"There! Do you see what I mean? Knowing that's how I feel about you, would you want me to marry you?"

"It could work, with patience."

"Yes. For you and Debbie, if you want it to."

"You know that's not what I meant."

"I know. But please, Fred, think it over. She's crazy about you. With me out of the picture, it could happen, if you'd let it."

They had almost reached the hibiscus hedge bordering the McCloud home and started to turn back when Fred said in a strangled voice, "I'll always remember how you looked today, when I finally realized you'll never marry me." The sweep of his arm seemed to include the bower of hibiscus behind them, the ohia trees with the red lehua blossoms, the honeycreepers warbling in their branches, and the scent-laden breeze. "You were always the most beautiful girl in the world, and to me you always will be."

Touched in spite of herself, Sylvie looked down and her hair fell forward on each side of her face, like a curtain over their past.

With trembling fingers, he parted her hair and raised her chin. Then he hugged her tightly.

For a moment there was no sound other than the distant revelry. Then, behind them, a man cleared his throat loudly. Fred released Sylvie and stood before her, his arms hanging at his sides,

Sylvie saw Steve walk through the hibiscus hedge. His face devoid of expression, he looked at the sky, the trees—anywhere but at her and Fred.

Without a word to either man, Sylvie raced toward Iolani's cottage, hair and skirt flying behind her like banners of distress. But as she neared the cottage, she decided she'd be better off in the crowd. She didn't want to talk to Fred or to Steve, and either might follow her if she took refuge inside. She had said all she had to say—to Steve when she threw the evidence at him the evening before, and to Fred just now.

She slipped into the crowd around the *imus*, where the men were digging the roasted pigs out of the sand like pirates unearthing buried treasure. As the canvas was cut away, steam billowed out, bearing the appetizing essence of the meat. The banana and ti leaves around the pigs were burned black. The coffee-colored skin of the pigs was crisp and sizzling. The noise of the crowd grew as everyone laughed and shouted in anticipation of the feast they had awaited all afternoon. Each pig was lifted onto a *papauaa*—a huge wooden platter of ancient design—and the carving began.

Debbie found Sylvie and squeezed her arm. "How did it go?"

"I told him how I felt, Deb, just what I'd written to him already."

Through the steam coming from the *papauaas*, Sylvie looked across to Fred, who seemed lost in contemplation. He smiled politely at an excited old Filipino woman who pointed something out to him.

"I have to talk to you," Debbie said.

Reluctant to leave the highlight of the luau, but hearing the urgency in her friend's voice, Sylvie asked, "Do you want to go to Iolani's house?"

"No, we don't need to. But let's back away from all this commotion so we can have some privacy."

They left the crowd around the *papauaas* and sat on the grass a short distance away.

"I'm going back to Oklahoma City." The expression on Debbie's pixie face showed that she dreaded Sylvie's reaction.

"What?" Sylvie couldn't hide her consternation. For a second all she could think of was her own situation. With no roommate to share expenses, and a job that at present was insecure to say the least, she felt alone and abandoned. Then she chided herself for her self-concern. Debbie must have had a terribly important reason for reaching such a momentous decision. She gave her friend her full attention.

"It must sound crazy to you," Debbie was saying, "but you know how I feel about Fred. I've never loved anyone like this. But now isn't the time to let him know. He has to get over you first."

"I told him."

"You didn't! How could you?"

"I felt he had to know. I didn't have any idea you were planning to go back, so I wanted to do something about it while he was here."

Debbie folded and unfolded her hands in her lap. "How can I look him in the face now? I'm so embarrassed."

"I certainly didn't mean to upset you. In fact I thought I was helping you. You and Fred are so much alike, and you always enjoyed each other when the three of us did things together. I'm surprised we all didn't realize before this that you're the right one for him."

"Well, I'm willing just to be his friend for now and see what happens." Debbie spoke slowly, as if finding her way through the fog of a dream. "I'm sorry you told him, because that makes it awkward, but I'm still going to carry out my plan."

"Which is . . . ?"

"He's hurt now, but, as you said, he'll get over it." Debbie's voice was soft with tenderness. "I want to be near him and be supportive. If his friendship doesn't turn into something else, at least I'll have tried."

"When are you going to give your notice at work?"

"I'm not going to give any notice. I'm going back right away, when he does."

For the first time since they had known each other, Sylvie saw her friend blush, but the set of her chin showed Debbie's determination.

"This is the most important thing in my life right now. I don't feel good about leaving without any notice, but that's exactly what I'm going to do."

"Maybe they'd still give you a reference if I took your job and filled in for you right away," Sylvie said impulsively.

"That'd be great. But what about your job at Steve's lab?"

"I forgot you didn't know—we haven't had a chance to talk since last night. I don't know if I have a job anymore, and even if I do, I don't know if I want it." Sylvie explained briefly about the patent, Steve's accusations, her own behavior, and Virginia's treachery.

"I never would have dreamed that Virginia would do such a thing! I can see why you felt you had to have proof. But where did you get the courage to break into her condo?" Debbie stared at her, then giggled. "I think the balmy air of the islands has turned both of us balmy too. I'm going to call my supervisor at home tonight and give her the news. Do you want me to recommend you?"

"Just give her my name and leave me her number. I'll call her after I get back to Honolulu. I can't avoid Steve much longer, but I don't want to get committed somewhere else until I hear what he has to say, since he's had time to think things over. I don't see how I can stay at the lab, but I do owe him a chance to apologize."

Debbie asked Sylvie to sell the Monza for her and said she'd leave the lease at their apartment. The rent on the carriage house was paid up till October, which relieved some of Sylvie's financial pressures. Debbie was planning to leave the Big Island on a late flight, and the next day she'd be flying back to Oklahoma with Fred. As from a great height, Sylvie watched her entire life changing, with absolutely no control over it. Surely Debbie, with her loving heart, her enthusiasm and determination, would be Fred's wife sometime in the future. And Sylvie herself . . . what was she doing? Drifting from job to job. In love with a man who didn't trust her, who had a mistress, and who was convinced that she loved someone else. He had overheard Fred's phone call at the laboratory, and after what he'd seen today, there would be no way to explain. Working in a hospital, as she had during her training, might make her feel secure again, on more familiar ground than on the shifting sands that claimed her now.

"Come on!" Mahina cried, running toward them. "Don't you know this is a party? You look too serious! Come on, everything's ready."

The three of them hurried toward the tables. Most of the seats were taken, and Mahina chided, "See, now you can't choose where you sit. You were over there jabbering away as if you hadn't seen each other in months."

"Over here!" Joe called from where he sat with two empty chairs between him and Iolani. "We've been saving these for you, and don't think it's been easy!"

"You two go on," Debbie told Sylvie and Mahina. "I'll find Fred." She hurried away with a spring in her steps, her lavender skirt and lei of vanda orchids bouncing to the rhythm of her joyful heart.

Despite the sequence of events that had rolled over her life like a rock slide, Sylvie had the resilience of youth and she was famished. This was her first luau and she was going to enjoy it. Besides the tender pork, aromatic with the flavor of ti leaves, there were butterfish and scallops, shrimp and clams, and a tasty dish of crushed kuku nuts baked with *paakia* salt. The flavors and aromas were so intriguing and varied that Sylvie soon stopped trying to sort them out, but she tried to sample everything.

She was drinking coconut through a straw straight from the coconut, when Joe handed her a mai tai. During the meal she hadn't let herself brood about Steve, but now, as she sipped the rum drink through a straw in a pineapple husk, he approached her table, so handsome in blue slacks and ivory knit shirt that she couldn't bear to meet his eyes.

He leaned over to whisper something to a young man across the table from her. The young man picked up his plate and, with a wide grin, moved to another table.

"Hello, Sylvie," he said evenly.

"Hello." She concentrated on twirling the straw in the pineapple husk.

"Steve McCloud," Iolani chirped, "it was about time you showed up at your own party."

"I've been here the whole time, Nanny."

"Then why didn't you come to see me?"

"Because I didn't want to be scolded, as you know very well," he told her. His light banter with Iolani gave no hint of the intensity with which he watched Sylvie.

"Yes, indeed I do," Iolani replied. "But you'll get a mighty scolding from me sometime very soon, and you know it."

"Not here!" he pleaded in mock consternation.

Her face broke into a thousand lines as she beamed at him and shook a finger in his direction.

"Where did you hide your boyfriend, Sylvie?" he asked. His face was inscrutable.

"What boyfriend?" asked Iolani, her head cocked to one side as she tried not to miss a word amid the merrymaking that surrounded them.

"Ask her, Nanny. Ask the girl who can make flowers tell lies."

Sylvie reached for the red hibiscus in her hair, but Iolani, with her intuition that surmounted her lack of sight, took her hand away and cautioned, "Don't be foolish, child."

"Iolani, I must go," Sylvie said. She couldn't bear to stay in Steve's presence. He had hurt her too much, and now he was needling her about Fred, without really caring for an explanation. Steve had made up his mind about her relationship with Fred, just as he had about her supposed lack of discretion about his research. He knew all the answers—and he was always wrong.

"Sylvie, look over there." Mahina pointed to where several women in short ti-leaf skirts were gathering. A group of men had started playing steel guitars, banjos, ukuleles, and all sorts of native percussion instruments, including split-bamboo rattles like the ones Muriel had used to accompany the lunchtime hula lessons.

"We'll have to be quick now," Mahina said. "Everything is starting and I want to join in right away. I found out the Maori farewell song and the 'Hawaiian Wedding Song' will be played near the beginning, and since those are the only dances I taught you, you won't want to be late. They're almost ready to begin."

"Mahina, I don't feel like dancing right now."

"Don't be silly. You know those two numbers to perfection. Once we start, you'll be dying to join in," Mahina replied cheerfully, pulling Sylvie along by the hand.

The two young women—one so dark, one so fair—rushed through their preparations in the small guest bedroom of Iolani's cottage. Off came the gathered skirts and peasant blouses, and on went two-piece swimsuits. Mahina's was white, in striking contrast to her dusky skin, and Sylvie's was blue.

"Isn't this pretty short?" Sylvie asked as she tied on the ti-leaf skirt. "It doesn't even come to my knees."

"It's the traditional hula costume. None of those plastic-grass skirts for us. You'll fit right in with the others."

As they brushed their hair, Sylvie asked, "What about flowers?"

"They'll have fresh leis for us there. Wreaths for our hair, too, to match the other dancers."

They hastened outside, their ti-leaf skirts swaying gently with the motion of their steps.

Sylvie's hand went to her necklace of green stones and she said, "What a combination of colors! Green necklace, ti-leaf skirt another shade of green, blond hair, red hibiscus, blue swimsuit . . . I must look like a rainbow!"

"Isn't a rainbow beautiful?" Mahina replied, hurrying toward the other dancers. "Look around you. Do you think the color of the grass clashes with the colors of the flowers growing everywhere?"

When the girls joined the other dancers, they were given red plumeria garlands and leis like those worn by the others. The musicians were playing a rhythmic song with a sweet-sad Hawaiian melody, then the strains of the "Hawaiian Wedding Song" began, and Sylvie followed Mahina to join the other dancers. As Mahina and the others smiled encouragement to her, she was unaware of the contrast she made with her petite figure, her fair skin with its even, honey-colored tan, and her luxuriant blond hair falling to her waist.

Her hips swayed with the music in the figure eight that Sylvie had practiced until it came so naturally that she didn't even have to think about it, while her bare feet moved lightly in time to the music, and her hands wove their story of love and fulfillment. The other dancers were all around her like brightly feathered birds, their hands and eyes telling the story more powerfully than any words could.

Sylvie danced and smiled, her eyes wandering over the crowd. She noticed Debbie and Fred in earnest conversation and hoped they would work things out between them. Then she saw the circle of spectators part deferentially to make way for Steve. He stood before her and watched her dance. She tried to avoid the power of his blue-green eyes, which seemed to draw her to him and reject her at the same time. What were those eyes trying to tell her? There was no smile on his lips. He stood still, straight and unmoving.

She smiled, as she was supposed to, and wanted to sing to him the words of the song, "I do, I do love you, with all my heart." But if she let herself do such a thing, there would be no response from him. The only thing to do was avoid looking at him, but that was impossible when she remembered dancing in his arms at the Surf Club to the music of this very song. She smiled while she danced, looking at Debbie, at Iolani, at Joe Lahine, even at Fred—anywhere but at Steve. It was no use. His eyes demanded hers again and again.

Now they were playing the Maori farewell song—"now is the hour that we must say goodbye"—the poignant words whirling in her mind. It was a sad song of good-bye, and Sylvie didn't have to smile anymore. Now she was dancing for Steve alone, saying her farewell, holding his eyes. She was bidding farewell to her foolish dream and weeping within, saying good-bye to what could have been and never would be. An overwhelming sadness filled her and she feared she might cry.

There would be no rainbow for her. She'd have to leave his laboratory; after the scene last night, she couldn't bear to work with him any longer.

The song was almost over when it happened. Slim and smart in a white tailored skirt with an emerald-green blouse, Virginia appeared at Steve's side and whispered something to him. He looked down at her and didn't move away when, flashing a triumphant glance at Sylvie, Virginia placed her hand on his tanned arm. Then they hurried away together, and Sylvie,

thankful when the song ended, fled toward Iolani's cottage.

Debbie ran after her and, seeing her tears,
cried, "What's the matter?"

"Nothing, Deb," she choked, "nothing at all."

"I was going to say good-bye. Fred and I have
to leave soon to catch our flight back, but I can't
leave you like this."

"There's nothing you can do, and anyway I
need to be alone right now. Say good-bye to Fred
for me, and good luck, dear friend." They embraced, then Sylvie ran on to the cottage, leaving Debbie standing there watching her.

In Iolani's guest room, Sylvie threw her ti-leaf
skirt, the lei, and the garland onto the bed, then
changed back into her skirt and blouse. She sat
for a moment on the bed, a picture of dejection,
with her head bowed, her hair falling around her
face, and her hands clasped in her lap. Then she
straightened. It wasn't fair. Virginia, who must
have made some explanation that satisfied
Steve, would marry him in spite of what she had
done. If Virginia truly loved him, Sylvie knew
she could bear the hurt more easily. But surely a
woman who did what Virginia had done to Steve
had no concept of what love could mean. Sylvie
loved him . . . oh so much. But where was her
pride? How could she love a man who didn't
trust her? She felt the hot indignation rising inside her like lava. She couldn't stand to look at
him, ever again—especially with Virginia at his
side.

Sylvie remembered Joe Lahine's jeep parked
in the driveway. The keys were in it, and he had
said she was welcome to use it. The festivities
would last well into the night, and no one would
miss her. Mahina would be with her fiancé,
Debbie and Fred were leaving, Steve was with
Virginia. As usual, all the world was paired, just

like on Noah's ark. Without a destination, knowing only that she couldn't bear to be so close to Steve, Sylvie drove off into the night.

She followed the road around the front of the McCloud mansion, and, just before turning onto the avenue lined with ohia trees, she looked back. Steve and Virginia were framed together in the lighted doorway, under the graceful columns of the southern-style plantation house. Sylvie brushed away her tears and stared straight ahead. The jeep seemed to have a will of its own. In less than an hour she found herself on Kilauea, without knowing how she had reached the rim of the crater. Passing the lookout where Steve had held her in his arms, she told herself that the memory of a few kisses should not have plunged her into this turmoil that she could neither understand nor control.

She parked the jeep and walked to the rim of the crater, where she stood gazing at the fire pit, which was thrown in sharp relief against the midnight-blue of the far walls of the crater. At her feet, the lava formations were eerie in the moonlight, casting distorted shadows and reflecting light like black diamonds. The waves of lava were as contorted as a vision of the underworld—a perfect landscape for the private hell pit she had dug for herself. Madame Pele was silent tonight. Not a spark flew from Halemaumau—the House of Everlasting Fire—and only a thin plume of steam, soon dispersed in the soft breeze, taunted her from the distance, as a ghostly hand beckoning her.

Sylvie descended into the crater. Loose lava, dislodged by her steps, rolled away under her feet, and the thumps reverberated with a dull echo from the sloping walls. She walked toward the craggy inner circle that stood guard around the fire pit. How long had she walked over the rough trail? She'd lost all notion of time. The effort of treading her way over the crumbly lava formations released some of her anger, but the hurt remained untouched within her breast, like a chunk of lava she couldn't dislodge.

When Sylvie began her ascent up the crags that enveloped the rim of the fire pit—the doorway to the house of the mythical Hawaiian goddess—she pulled off her necklace and called up toward the rim, "I don't believe you exist! You're just an old hole in a mountain, spilling your boiling guts over the earth!"

". . . earth . . . earth . . ." the echo mocked her.

Another sound—a sound of falling rocks, menacing in this lunar landscape—answered the echo. From the edge of the crater, chunks of lava tumbled, one upon the other, with the sound of distant drums. Sylvie stood by the fire pit and looked whence she had come. There was nothing she could see in the shadows cast by the walls of the crater where the moonlight didn't penetrate. Perhaps some pieces of lava, dislodged by her own descent, were only now tumbling down.

She had resumed her ascent and was nearly at the top of the fire pit when she saw a man running toward her. Her heart thumped loudly when she recognized Steve's light shirt, bright in the moonlight, and his lope across the floor of the crater.

"Sylvie!" he called. "Wait!"

". . . wait . . . wait . . ." the echo entreated.

"What for?" she shouted back. To be hurt again? To fool herself into believing that there was a chance he might care for her? No! She was through with him. She never wanted to see him again. She hurried up the side of the fire pit and stood outlined in the silvery glow of the waning moon.

Steve had reached the foot of the tumbled rocks and he called up to her, "I'm sorry. I'm sorry for everything. For misjudging you. For mistreating you. For accusing you. For giving you no chance to explain." He hurried after her.

"Go away and let me be! Every time you have a doubt about anything at all, you immediately think the worst. I want nothing to do with you. Go back to your mistress and leave me alone!" she cried.

He reached her side and stood looking down at her, stretching his arms toward her.

She backed away and raised her hand, ready to throw the necklace into the fire pit, which was so dark and silent tonight. "This is what I think of the stupid necklace. Just a piece of junk that belongs to Pele, that cruel, mocking figment of the imagination."

He grabbed her hand and took the necklace, then stuffed it into his pocket. "Please, Sylvie, let me explain."

She bit her lip and took another step backward. If only he could explain away all her hurt and melt away the lump in her chest.

He stood watching her, not coming closer, as if he were afraid she would run away from him if he startled her. "I was unjust. I knew it immediately after I hung up last night."

"My feelings don't matter to you! All you care about is getting credit for your discovery. Mahina and I did the best we could to safeguard your patent. It's not our fault if—"

"Sylvie, please. The patent is safe. The attorney will submit our evidence and an interference will be declared."

"But you couldn't bother to answer your

phone and let me know. I expect you didn't want me to intrude on your tête-à-tête with that . . . that . . ."

"Darling, please!"

"Well, isn't that so?" Just as the curt words were flung at him, she realized he had called her "darling." She felt as if the chunk of lava she carried in her chest was melting, like molten lava spreading warmth all through her body. Her heart, which she had hardened against him, fluttered and started beating wildly. She wanted him to take her into his arms; instead, still afraid of the hurt he could inflict on her if she let him know how vulnerable she was, she looked down, the curtain of her hair descending to shield her face.

"There's been nothing at all between Virginia and me since I brought you to this island—to this volcano. *Nothing*, do you hear? Just as there has been nothing between you and that fellow—Fred—since then. But I didn't know, just as you didn't. Since I overheard your phone conversation with him at the lab, I've been wild with jealousy. I lashed out at you about the patent when what I really wanted was to lash out at you about him. I couldn't bear the thought of another man touching you. Of you caring for anyone else but me." He looked away and admitted in a voice so soft that Sylvie could barely hear him, "Iolani set me straight about that."

Sylvie raised her head and looked at him, still keeping her distance. His eyes looked like the fathomless silvery night, holding the secret of her happiness. "But you brought her to the luau!" she insisted.

"I did not! She came of her own accord to try to explain her way out. I let her talk. Then I had my say. She understands that she needn't report back to work on Monday—or ever again."

A tiny smile turned up the corners of Sylvie's mouth. He was saying all the things she had longed to hear. He was soothing away all the pain and longing of these past weeks.

Steve opened his arms and she walked into them. Crushing her to his chest, he murmured in the silk of her hair, "You mean more to me than I ever believed another human being could mean. I love you, Sylvie."

She raised her face to him, and he bent down to kiss her lips, her hair, her eyes, again and again, as if she were a magic potion that alone could sustain his life. She lost herself in his kisses, encircled by the fire of his arms, responding as she never had before, without holding back.

When he let her go, she felt giddy, as if she'd had too much to drink. He pulled the necklace out of his pocket and slipped it around her neck. "Your good luck charm," he teased. "Only it worked in slow motion. Think of the time we've wasted. And it's really all my fault. Right after we kissed on the lookout, you behaved like a startled doe, and I decided then that I should tread carefully and not frighten you away from me again. I knew then I wanted you for my own—forever."

She leaned her head against his chest. "I thought you lost all interest when you found out I was going to be one of your employees."

"No, darling. I only knew that I would have to be doubly cautious and gentle. I only backtracked. It was just one more complication, but I never had any intention of giving you up. Never." Again he enfolded her in his strong arms in the throbbing night, and she lost all awareness of time.

"Here, let me set this right," he said at last. He smiled down at her in the light of the moon, which, for Sylvie, now shone brighter than any sun. He took the red hibiscus from her hair and gently repinned it behind her right ear. "Now, let's go back to the luau so everyone can see that my lady is unavailable to anyone but her husband-to-be."

ABOUT THE AUTHOR

LUCINDA DAY is a Kansas wife and mother with a wide range of interests—from travel to gourmet cooking, reading, breeding Dobermans, swimming, camping, bird watching, playing the piano and teaching creative writing. Lucinda is also the author of another Circle of Love romance, *Gates of the Sun.*

CIRCLE OF LOVE ™

**Step out of your world
and enter the
Circle of Love**

Six new CIRCLE OF LOVE romances are available every month. Here's a preview of the six new titles coming next month:

#28 PRELUDE TO HAPPINESS by Angela Petron

A marvelous trip to Finland was Emma's if she would pretend to be Martin's fiancee. But Emma wanted the love to be real.

#29 ONCE AND FOREVER by Maeve Fitzgerald

Had Alex come to see Hillary to flaunt the wild affair that shattered their love? Or was it to recapture the passion Hillary still held in her heart?

#30 THE HADLEIGH INHERITANCE by Alethia Hunt

An instant heiress, Rosemary was swept into a world of twisted family secrets, searching for a legacy of love.

#31 A TIME FOR ALL SEASONS by Megan Lefey

William's sudden, dark moods bewildered Rachel. But he aroused in her a passion she never knew before.

#32 THE SHELTERED HAVEN by Patt Parrish

How could Rachel ignore the painful memories Alex brought back? And how could she keep herself from opening her heart again?

#33 A LIGHT IN THE VALLEY by Mary Mackie

Could Jan endure Neil's unpredictable passion? Or should she risk her heart on the gentle, yet unapproachable Philip?

Read all of these Circle of Love books, available wherever Bantam paperbacks are sold.